AN ANTIQUE CHRISTMAS

AN ANTIQUE CHRISTMAS

BY: SHERI POWROZEK

DEDICATION

As the icy-cold, opaque snow hits the ground, as your boots pass through its iridescent and powdery resonance, as it hits your face just so, coming down from the heavens with perfect grace to cover everything in a blanket-like effect, casting its beauty upon us, we are blessed with its Christmas glow. The children laugh with glee, and animals frolic about, playfully taking it in. We bundle up and prepare ourselves for the cold winter ahead, while embracing the holidays, full of love, warmth, and joy.

This book is dedicated to family. Every single member that makes up a unit. To every memory. To every gathering. To every friend. To every kind soul that gives themselves to the world with selflessness.

Celebrate the simple, little moments, and cherish the blessings. Marinate in the wonderous and blissful moments of what is. Merry Christmas, from our house to yours.

TABLE OF CONTENTS

Chapter 1: A New York Proposition

Twisted garland, white twinkle lights, and wreaths of pinecone with red bows covered the banquet hall. Addison Monroe stirred her drink and ate the cherry garnish it was adorned with. An echo from the microphone bellowed through the gathering as Christmas karaoke continued to ensue. Jim Hawkins, from accounting, was singing a new version of "Silent Night," making the mood melancholy, like a dose of melatonin, putting the room to sleep. Yawning and trying to stay in the holiday spirit, Addison walked past the tables of food and picked up a few toothpicks of cheese, trying to avoid the greasy, fried appetizers that were laid out before her. She could sense someone lurking over her shoulder. She was startled by the depth of his voice as he spoke to her.

"Why don't you join Jim up there?" Greyson Herrington suggested, eyeing her up and down, taking her in and letting it be known that he was interested. Subtlety wasn't his strong suit. He was overly confident with an air of cockiness about him. His eyebrows were raised, his mouth flicking up into a smirk. Anything Greyson wanted, he got. He had looks, money, and clout.

With a tilt of her head and a raise of the eyebrows, Addison gave him a look of disinterest. "No, thank you."

His cologne carried the scent of pine and old spice, and it was heavily doused upon his body, overwhelming her sense of smell, giving her

1

an instant headache. She winced and stopped herself from sneezing, turning away from him for a moment and taking in a deep breath. Addison knew he was a bigwig from corporate headquarters. She recognized him from commercials and advertisements. He was the face of Doxens, the largest retail fashion outlet in New York. She wanted to make a good impression, since he was a main figure in their company, but she wasn't in the mood to entertain him.

Pushing himself on her further, he stepped closer, placing his hand upon her shoulder. "Come on. What's your favorite Christmas carol?" he prodded.

Pulling away, Addison politely smiled. "I like all the traditional jingles, but that doesn't mean I want to go up there and sing them, embarrassing myself."

Unamused and not taking no for an answer, he put his hand upon her shoulder, once again. "You can't come to the holiday office party and not have regrets in the morning. That's part of the memo. You say and do embarrassing things, making your co-workers and boss notice you. Then, there are stories for years to come about you." Greyson chuckled. He was taken with himself. He bounced back and forth to the music, while snapping his fingers. "Just stay by me, and you will have a good time. I know how to work a crowd."

She stared at him curiously. The only thing that came to the forefront of her mind was the word narcissist. He was nothing short of the definition. She slightly giggled over his demeanor. "It's in the memo, huh?" Addison asked with disbelief.

"Just going off personal experience. A few years back, I knocked over the Christmas tree while dancing to 'Jingle Bell Rock.' Now, I'm legend. Ask anyone," he said.

"So, you are the one. I've heard about that infamous incident. Pretty impressive. Since you give such great advice, I suggest you go up first. You can show me how it's done." Addison winked at him and suggestively pointed at the stage.

"In due time," he said with a sly smile.

Addison wasn't impressed with his overly cocky attitude. She was keeping an eye on the clock until Mr. Lambert did MVP awards and gave away Christmas bonuses. She wanted nothing more than a bonus check and a swift exit, so she could go home and lounge in her cotton pajamas and binge on Christmas movies.

"Truffle?" Greyson asked, putting his hand out. A chocolate ball rested upon his palm for her to take.

Reaching out, she grabbed it and took a bite. "Thank you." Covering her mouth with her hand, embarrassed that she probably had fudge in her teeth, Addison took a sip of water and wiped her face with a napkin.

A vibration from Addison's coat pocket grabbed her attention. Reaching her hand inside the pocket, she pulled out her phone to read a text that came through.

SANDRA: I locked up the house. I put the keys for the shop on the hook in the laundry room. Good luck, dear.

It was from Sandra, her mother's housekeeper. Sadness came over Addison, depleting her spirit of happiness. She put her phone back in her pocket, grabbed a glass of champagne off a serving tray, and downed its bubbly concoction in two gulps. Then, she took a napkin and piled on the greasy appetizers that she was avoiding, to fill the incessant need of comfort and warmth that she longed for. The waiter came back around, and she grabbed another glass of champagne, mimicking the same action as moments before.

Noticing her change in demeanor, Greyson stepped in front of her and met her eye to eye. "Whoa. Did you have a change of heart? Drinking at that rate, I assume you will be up there before me. You okay?"

"I'm having a rough day. I have to go home for Christmas, something I am not looking forward to," she admitted.

"That bad, huh?" he prodded. "Usually Christmas is a happy time."

"Yeah, usually it is, but I would like to forget about it tonight. This year might be a somber and lonely one."

"Then, how about a Christmas cookie espresso shooter? It tastes like a snickerdoodle and gives you a burst of energy," Greyson said.

"Sure, why not, I could use the caffeine. I didn't have my coffee today," she answered.

"No baking required," Greyson joked. He laughed so hard at his own candor, Addison was amused. She had never met anyone that was more taken with themselves than him.

Greyson grabbed two mini glass shooters from the server's tray and handed the caramel colored drink to Addison. "Ready. On the count of three. One, two, three."

Addison and Greyson stared at each other during the countdown, clinked the sides of their glasses together, and downed the sugary flavors at once. For a brief second, Addison's eyes took to his, noticing how handsome and entrancing he was. His eyes were coyote brown with flecks of honey. His hair was full, sandy brown, and perfectly combed.

Hmm...he is quite handsome, she thought.

The sound of his voice broke her stare. "I enjoy you. There's something simple yet unorthodox about you. Your face is so pure and distinct. I think you should be on the next campaign with me. You would be perfect. I've been looking for someone that stands out from the rest but in a non-traditional way. It would be refreshing to have someone that I can collaborate with that can carry their own ideas and has natural flow to their repertoire, representing the company when they are by themselves in public. Often times, we get spotted out on the town, and we have to think fast and keep up a good reputation for the brand. Something tells me you would be perfect at that." Greyson raised his eyebrows up and down to let her know that he was serious. Then, he continued. "I spend long hours with my modeling partner. I'd prefer to enjoy myself, rather than not."

Staring at him with widened eyes, she didn't know if she should believe him or let it go. Thoughts started swirling in her head. *Is this a ploy to get me to go home with him? Me? On a billboard?* Addison was shocked. *He thought I could be a model?* The sugar must have gone to his head.

5

Addison couldn't figure out why he was still talking with her and what kept him so interested. She was just an account executive, a good girl; simplistic, innocent, and pure, nothing fancy.

She pushed the subject to see how serious he was. "I've never really thought of it before. I'm used to being behind the scenes."

"You don't belong behind the scenes. You belong front and center. I think we would look great together, and we could produce some quality work," he insisted with confidence.

Addison blushed. *Is this a line? Is this what he says to every girl?* she pondered. Then, she stared at him for a brief second before responding. "Hmm...well, I will be out of town for a little bit over the holiday. Will you put in a good word for me, so when I come back we can approach the idea together? I could use some time to think."

"All I have to do is say something. I can suggest whatever I want. I know Mr. Lambert; he will approve. He trusts my opinion. Besides, my face gives this business a lot of money. If it wasn't for me, he wouldn't have reached the sales he did this year. I have contacts and a large fanbase. He knows it. So, if I want you as my campaign partner, he should be more than willing to oblige. He will love that you are already a part of the company. Promoting from within is one of his mottos. But let's just agree that you have to go out with me first. New Year's Eve... be my date? When you get back?" Greyson waited for her to respond.

Addison was a bit uncomfortable, knowing that he had conditions and expectations. "I don't normally go out on New Year's Eve," she answered politely. She didn't want to tell him that she wasn't really interested in pursuing a romantic connection if they were going to work together so closely. She didn't want to blur the lines. Yet, she knew he could be an integral part in furthering her career. And as she stared back into his light amber browns, she felt his good looks soften her. He was quite captivating. A friendly dinner between the two of them couldn't hurt. Her voice stuttered a little bit, but before she could get her final answer out, Greyson interrupted.

"Don't think too hard. It sounds like you might need a good pick me up when you get back, just a fun time, no pressure. How about it?" he persisted.

"When you put it that way, sure. New Year's it is," Addison confirmed with a coy smile. She could easily cancel if she changed her mind by then, but she didn't want to let the opportunity pass her by. Even though, now that she said yes, all she could think about was the midnight kiss. Would he be expecting it? Would it mean anything? Should she bow out?

Greyson cleared his throat. "Now that I got that out of the way, if you don't mind, I'm going to excuse myself. I feel the microphone calling my name."

"Don't let me hold you back. By all means, go for it," Addison cheered him on. Lightly clapping her hands, she joined the crowd in watching him take the stage.

His presence dominated, partly because he was full of himself and his ego entered the room before he did, but also because he had an over-the-top, in your face persona, that most people couldn't look away from, attracting everyone's eyes and ears with his dashing good looks. Greyson began reciting the melody to "Blue Christmas" by Elvis Presley. Changing his voice lower and deeper to mimic the historical legend, he began moving his upper lip, eyebrow, and hips, getting in full character.

Addison couldn't help but chuckle at his dorky imitation. She was one of the few women in the room that could see right through him. She liked a more subdued, silent confidence about her suitors. However, she did find him quite entertaining, seeing that he wasn't afraid to make a fool of himself. It was refreshing.

Greyson started pointing in Addison's direction, signaling her to join him. As the crowd turned toward her, she grew self-conscious and immediately shook her head no. She felt a sweat break out on her forehead from the attention, giving her anxiety. He winked at her and stayed consistent in his attempts. As he finished that song and began a new one, he stopped what he was doing. He took a step off stage and put his hand out to her, waiting for her to come and place her hand in his. He put his mouth to the microphone. "I need a partner for this one. It's a duet. Addison, please join me."

Addison didn't budge. Greyson waved her forward. She looked mortified as the entire room egged it on.

"Go on, Addison, join him," shouted Hillary from Marketing.

"Yep, C'mon up here. Sing with me. I'm waiting," Greyson requested.

With apprehension, Addison forced a smile and began walking towards him to join him on stage. With a sheepish grin, she took her hands out of her dress pockets and looked into his eyes as he awaited her. Putting her hand in his, he helped her up the stairs. Turning around to face everyone, she stood with the spotlight gleaming into her eyes, blinding her. Squinting, she put her hand up by her forehead to shield her eyes from the brightness. Her face was flushed, and her heart was beating fast, barely keeping a steady breath. Concentrating, she held the microphone tightly with both hands, quietly adding her voice as a background harmony to "White Christmas," trying to remember the words, letting Greyson take the lead. He had a soft, raspy, soulful voice. Knowing it was her solo coming up, she cleared her throat. A country twang hit her vocal chords in just the right way, taking the next line. Her voice was in exact range and key, elegant and refined. Greyson looked at her with awe, realizing she had a soothing and brilliant voice. Their voices, unique in their own ways, came together perfectly, staying in sync and complimenting the other. They began to sing the chorus together and set an upbeat, cheerful, holiday spirit about the room. Seeing the crowd's reaction, listening to the background instruments, and knowing they were in tune, Addison smiled grandly, swaying back and forth. Greyson didn't take his eyes off her. The crowd grew interested in their connection and chanted for them to sing another. Addison was already uncomfortable with so much attention and didn't think she could do any more. She bowed out gracefully.

"Thank you." She gave a curtsy and handed the microphone back to Greyson.

A loud applause came over the room.

He gave her a sad look. "Already? Really? Not even one more song? How about, 'Baby It's Cold Outside?' 'Rockin' Around the Christmas Tree?' 'Chestnuts Roasting on an Open Fire?' Name it, and we can sing it."

"No, really, I'm not sure my heart can handle another spotlight moment." Addison laughed. She moved off the stage to the corner of the room, sitting down at a table and removing herself from the chaos. Being an introvert, panic set in as she realized she had taken part in such an escapade. The crowd gave a light boo to show their dismay, and Greyson threw his arms up in the air.

Addressing the audience, Greyson put his mouth closer to the microphone. "Well, guys, I tried." He continued on and sang "Let it Snow."

Mortified, Addison tried hiding her face. A waiter came by and set down a cup. "Tea?" he asked.

"Oh, yes, please."

As he poured the steaming hot beverage into her mug and the aroma of green leaves and lemon filled up the air, she was delighted to enjoy a warm drink and hoped it would relax her. She turned toward the waiter. "Thank you."

He looked at her and smiled. "You are very welcome. And may I say, you have quite the voice."

Addison blushed and shook her head. "That's kind of you. I appreciate you saying that."

He nodded and walked away.

Greyson finished up two more songs, full of dance moves and spins, keeping the room energized. He was joined by other colleagues that were mesmerized by him. Addison could tell he was enjoying the fan-dome. He lived for it.

At the end of "Silver Bells," Mr. Lambert walked on stage and playfully stole the microphone. "Here, here, now, that's enough for the night. I'm not sure we can handle anymore karaoke. And I would like to cut this night short before we have repeated shenanigans of the years past."

The room filled with laughter, and Greyson gave the crowd a mischievous smile.

Mr. Lambert patted him on the back and then paid recognition to Greyson and his Vice President, Larry Seywall. Together, Greyson and Larry gave a nice speech thanking Mr. Lambert for giving them global opportunities and promotions. For their hard work, Mr. Lambert gave them an extra bonus and a paid vacation to the Greek Isles.

Wouldn't that be nice, Addison thought.

She had been with Doxens for three years, interning and then full-time, and had never received a trip. A measly one dollar raise and a two hundred and fifty-dollar Christmas bonus was all she could muster up with the likes of him. He didn't even know her name. He usually confused her with a girl named Mallory, who worked in the graphic arts sector. Addison thought it was silly to correct him so many times, so after a while, she gave up and accepted the nickname. But she knew that she wasn't going to move up the ladder if he was that oblivious to her. The only time she saw him was at corporate get-togethers and during quarterly reports, so it was hard to

11

get his attention and make an impact. Usually, she dealt with Larry. Seeing the perks Greyson and Larry got being at the top of the company made her envious. Greyson's suggestion to be on the next campaign sounded more appealing by the minute. Next year, she could be standing up there with him, receiving a trip around the world, receiving all the money she could dream of. Imagining it in her mind, she could picture herself dining in fancy restaurants, yachting, and attending red carpet events. Anything sounded better than being stuck in a cubicle and doing everyone's grunt work. Addison had always dreamt of having a successful career and living in a high-rise apartment with a doorman. She wanted to be respected and seen as a leader to all of her peers.

As everyone started to scatter and go home for the night, she wanted to make sure that Greyson saw her and remembered their earlier conversation. Walking up behind him, she tapped him on his shoulder, interrupting one of his conversations. He turned around and noticed her, giving her a flirtatious smile.

"Addison. Hey."

"Hey. Good job up there," she sweetly complimented.

"I wish you would have stayed with me. Instead, I had to deal with office groupies," he said with dislike.

"Hey, now. Most people would link me to that group. I work with most of them on a daily basis, so be nice. But it must feel good that they are enamored with you."

"Eh...I can't really blame them. No one can resist my dance moves," Greyson boasted.

Taking in his narcissistic, self-centered personality, Addison kept her feelings in and controlled her eyes from rolling. She wanted to puke, thinking about his conceited comments. "So, I'm about to go home. I just want to make sure we are on the same page. New Year's Eve, right? We are for sure getting together? I will talk to you before then and work out the details?" Addison asked.

"Of course. Unless you want to make it earlier and hang out tonight? My place?" Greyson stood there, refined, dapper, and completely sure of himself, with no thought towards rejection. He was playing it smooth, not realizing that Addison wasn't that type of girl.

Addison was in shock and a bit disgusted that he would think so little of her. "I really can't. I'm leaving early in the morning. I need to get my rest. We can talk soon."

He sighed. "Okay, your loss. I will have my assistant get ahold of you to square away the details. Good luck, and Merry Christmas." He buttoned his suit jacket and walked away, looking for the next best thing, putting his arm around anyone that welcomed it.

"You too. Merry Christmas," Addison uttered behind him.

Happy to leave, Addison said her last goodbyes and called a taxi to go home. Thinking over the night, she was enthusiastic about the future possibilities. Seeing a billboard in Times Square for Doxens and an up-close picture of Greyson with some beautiful, buxom blonde, she grew excited

13

and curious, dreaming about what theirs would look like. She wondered how they would be perceived and where it would take her. Maybe she would get to travel more and see the world? It was something to think about, especially now that she was completely on her own, with no one to depend on. With no real family keeping her in one place, she could go anywhere. It seemed a bit depressing but also freeing.

Her mother's death wasn't a complete surprise, but it happened quickly. Too quickly that Addison didn't get to see her in-person to say goodbye. She knew her mom loved her, and words were spoken between them that acknowledged their sentiments for one another, but it wasn't enough. There was a longing and a loneliness that she felt deep within, pulling at her heart. Addison would never be able to feel a warm embrace from her mother again. She would have to live with that guilt for the rest of her life. Knowing that she was going back to her childhood home to pack up her mother's belongings and close her antique store, Addison had mixed feelings of sadness and regret.

The last five years, Addison had been rather selfish. She focused solely on school, work, and her independence, leaving little room for people in her life. It made her question who she was as a person. What kind of life did she really have, neglecting the most important person to her? Besides meeting in the middle at one of their favorite restaurants, Addison and her mother didn't spend much time together, and now there would be no new memories to relish in. So much time had passed, and Addison blamed herself for wasting all of it. She thought her mom would always be there. She would give anything to turn the clock back and re-do things. How could she be so selfish, keeping her mom at a distance? Her mom deserved more, and she would never get a chance to tell her. Going back to Connecticut, she knew that she would be confronting it all. Whether she could handle what awaited her was yet to be seen.

Chapter 2: Stepping Back in Time

It had been years since Addison had stepped foot in the town of Edgerton. Faded memories came to the forefront of her mind, as if she was staring into a looking glass, vividly remembering voices, laughing, and playing from her youth. How had it been this long since she had visited? Regret plagued her once again, thinking about how much time went by and all the hours she'd wasted.

Stepping out of her car, as her gym shoes hit the pavement, she felt grounded in more ways than one. Deep rooted in the history of everything that surrounded her, she felt nostalgic and connected, while also feeling so separate, as it was no longer a part of her. She smiled, thinking of the last time she was home. She was just a teenager, a high school graduate, young and free. She didn't even know who she was then. Maybe she still didn't? Being back created a softness within her that pulled at her spirit. She always thought she'd outgrown the town, but she was now realizing that the town outgrew her. She was a confused, lost soul, and she needed to find herself. Back then, she didn't appreciate the town's charm, history, and majestic nature. As she stood there looking around, it was as if Edgerton was right out of a storybook, pulling her in and giving her the feels. It had a quaint, small town feel. There was a warmth, a peacefulness, and a happiness to Edgerton. The air felt light, pure, and refreshing. The stillness of the environment kept her in a relaxed state as adrenaline and anxiety tried taking over her body.

As a child, the little quirks and special characteristics of Edgerton were things she grew to dislike, because her curiosity and imagination soared, always thinking there were brighter and better things out there. She craved adventure, travel, and diversity. Being back, she realized how rare it was. Those little characteristics were what made it so unique and special.

Addison walked up the driveway and followed the sidewalk to the little white gate. The white, two-story craftsman house held its 1890's character. The cobblestone walkway, red brick accents, stark white wrap around with strong mahogany boards, and the large distressed blue entry door, immediately took her back to her adolescence. Tingling sensations shot up her back and down her arms as she imagined times of the past, when her mother sat on the porch swing or rocked in her favorite Adirondack chair. Addison made her way up the steps and placed her hand upon the railing, thinking of some of her fondest memories when she was just a little girl. She thought about her childhood; reading books, napping on her mom's lap, singing, and playing with her dolls. It was a flash of memory that brought up heavy emotion within her. Her lips began to tremble; her cheeks started to flush, and her eyes filled up, glossed over. Not wanting to be too emotional, she snapped herself back into her somber reality. Realizing that she would never experience that vision again and that her mom was gone, she let out a deep sigh, collecting herself and wiping her eyes before moving forward. Times were changing, life was moving swiftly, and it seemed like it was all passing her by.

Addison unzipped her purse to grab the house keys. She fiddled around, searching for them, but they got lost among the numerous receipts, make-up items, pens, and loose change that were scattered together on the bottom. A sweat came over her as she became frustrated. Her brows furrowed, and she grew tense, letting out a stressed huff, feeling overwhelmed emotionally. Stomping her foot and closing her eyes, she tried to regain her cool. Centering herself and calming down, she removed her wallet and found the keys underneath. Holding them in-between her fingers, she felt hesitant to enter. For a brief moment, she placed her hand around the bronze, circular doorknob and closed her eyes, saying a small prayer. As she turned the key and the door creaked open, a familiar scent surrounded her. With one breath, she was overtaken by it. The smell of her mom, the smell of her past, of her childhood, of all her memories … It was like the smell of an old shirt or blanket. Yet, the happiness that used to fill the house, the welcoming and warm spirit that embraced its walls, was now obsolete. The only thing it now inhabited were things: décor, artifacts, personal objects, and mementos. A stark loneliness crept in, making her feel cold.

Knowing her mother was sick and knowing she wouldn't make it, Addison thought it would lessen the grief, that it would somehow make it less painful having anticipated it. But nothing prepared her for the feelings she had in this moment. Being surrounded by her things, her smell, her life, it was harder than she imagined. In that exact moment, it became real. There was no one to call, no one to visit, no one to check on her. Her mom was gone. Picking up a picture frame from the front entry table, Addison held it in her hands, feeling the smooth leather upon it. A smile burst across her face as tears filled the inlets of her eyes. As much as she tried to suppress it, she couldn't stop the emotion. Her body filled with a bubbling up sensation, feeling sadness and stress. A heat came over her in her face and chest. She felt a burning, achy feeling near her heart. It hurt, like it was being tugged at. The picture was from Easter a few years back. She and her mom had met in Willshire, midway between their towns, for a short brunch. The looks on their faces were blissful. A day full of humor, catching up, and telling old stories. She wished more than anything that she could be back there, repeating that day. One more talk, one more hug, one more laugh, one more moment of hearing her voice and seeing her face. Until now, she didn't fully acknowledge just how much she needed and wanted that.

Addison's mother, Mona, was a soft-spoken, kind-hearted woman with a gentleness about her. She was very welcoming and friendly, opening her arms to anyone that needed it. To many, they would say she was a "light", a calming, happy lady that people wanted to be around. And even though she desperately wanted Addison to move back home from New York after she graduated NYU, she knew that Addison's happiness and rise to success was most important. Mona never wanted to ruffle feathers or make a big deal about things, and she wanted the very best for her daughter. Mona knew that Addison always dreamt of a life that was grander than Edgerton, and she never wanted to hinder that. She was there if Addison needed her, but she wanted Addison to make her own decisions that fit with her dreams. Maybe deep down, her motherly intuition knew something like this would happen, and Addison would need to be self-sufficient.

As Addison put the picture down and looked around, she felt a vibration in her pocket. She pulled her phone out and answered.

"Hello?"

A high-pitched voice pierced her eardrum. "Hi. Is this Addison?"

"Uh, yes. Yes, this is."

"Hi, Addison. This is Hannah. Greyson Herrington told me to contact you to set up a photo shoot. He also wanted me to get a date set on the calendar for New Year's Eve."

Addison sighed and closed her eyes. "Ugh," she grumbled quietly. Recollecting herself, she brought her voice back to a chipper tone. "Oh, yes. That's right. Sorry, you took me off guard. You know, I am actually in the middle of something, can I call you back?"

"Um … sure. I guess. I normally like to fulfill Mr. Herrington's requests. If you could get back to me by the end of the day, I would appreciate it. He doesn't like to wait."

"I'm sure he doesn't," Addison mumbled with attitude.

"Excuse me? What did you say? I didn't quite understand you."

"Nothing. Sorry. I will get back to you."

"Okay, Addison. Talk soon."

"Yep. Thanks. Bye." Addison let out another grumble as she hung up.

After placing the phone down on the table so she didn't get any more disruptive phone calls, Addison walked the perimeter of the house. She walked through every room, touching all of her mother's things. She picked up an old sweater from the bannister and put it up to her nose. It smelled like her body spray, a mix of guava and mango. An instant smile came across her face. Addison walked past the piano in the corner of the living room and slowly dragged her fingers across each key. Recalling it as if it was yesterday, the song "You are My Sunshine" played through her head. She sang the lyrics quietly as she played the first few notes.

"You are my Sunshine, My only Sunshine …"

It was a song that she had sang with her mom since she was a toddler. A cool feeling came over her, and she felt a light tickle upon the back of her neck. The warmth of the memory made her smile.

"Mom, if that's you, hi."

It was eerily quiet and lonely. The sun beams hit above the piano onto the wall, making it extremely bright.

She laughed at the thought, and then shook her head, knowing it was a crazy idea. Addison put the sweater on to keep warm and cuddled up in it.

What am I going to do now? Where am I going to start? How do I even know what she would want me to do with everything? Addison thought.

Overwhelmed, Addison thought it best to unpack her things, making herself comfortable. Then she would go into town. Going up the winding stairs, she carried her suitcase and found her way into her old bedroom. She placed her suitcase down on the chair in the corner, opened the curtains, and sat upon the edge of the bed. *Wow. Life is so funny. It sure is surprising. I have no more parents.* As she pondered about her life, feeling depressed, she got up and straightened her shirt, not allowing herself to wallow. *Get it together.* On the nightstand was a note with her name. Bewildered, she opened it slowly. It was in Sandra, the housekeeper's, writing.

Addison,

Before your mother passed, she wrote this down for you.

My dearest Addy,

Anything that was mine is now yours. Do what you want with everything but know that every item has a story. Don't be upset with me. I love you.

Mom

Addison scrunched up her face, furrowing her brows and sucking in her lips. *What did she mean? How could I be upset with her?* Confusion surrounded the note. Now, she was really nervous about what she would find and what she should do with all of her things. She almost wished she didn't have to take care of it all. It was too great a burden to bear. Her mother's things had been sacred to her. She didn't want this responsibility. Were there secrets her mom had been hiding? Was she in debt? Was she in trouble? She thought it over for a minute but then shook her head no. Not her mother. Her mother lived a simple and responsible life. Folding up the note, she opened a drawer in the nightstand and put it inside. Closing it, she went over to the chair with her things and unzipped her bag. Pulling out an undershirt and a flannel button down, she changed her shirt and got ready to head out. It was surreal moving about the house, as she once did as a child. It felt like a distant, faded movie trying to play out in her head. Yet, some things felt so familiar that they brought her right back. She remembered running up and down the hallways, giggling as her dad chased her. Playing hide and go seek in the closets. Having sleepovers with her friends. Spending long nights cuddling up to her mother in bed and reading stories or having deep conversations about boy problems.

She had a hard time walking past her mom's room. Peeking in, she took a deep breath. But as she exhaled, her chest went into convulsions. Overwhelming emotions took over her body, and she let out an exasperated shriek. Tears flooded her eyes and rolled down her cheeks. Her eyes burned, and her throat became dry and scratchy. She couldn't control herself; the heartache was too great. It burned in her chest again, but this time, it left her unable to breathe. Trying to control herself, she gasped with each breath. Sniffling, she went to her mother's dresser and grabbed a Kleenex. Addison hadn't felt grief like this since she was seventeen, when her father died.

The feeling was like nothing else she had ever experienced: complete darkness, sadness, anxiety, debilitating heart break, uncontrollable sobbing, and crippling pain in her heart and soul. It was something that still haunted her. She remembered it vividly. The sirens in her driveway, the police showing up at her door, her mom falling to the ground. It was unexpected and tragic. A heart attack that no one could have predicted. He was young and healthy. It came out of nowhere. He left for work like any other day. Yet, this day, he didn't make it. His body gave out, and he hit an oncoming vehicle, dead on scene. It was a memory that was ingrained in her brain, that was still traumatic to her soul. Part of her childhood slipped away that day. Her best friend left the world, and she didn't even get to say goodbye. No words, no hugs, no explanation. For a long time, she held a deep, residual resentment towards the world, feeling sorry for herself, not understanding why it happened to her. What was the lesson in all of it?

Addison's dad was extremely likeable and uncanny with his charm. No one ever knew exactly what he was thinking or what he was going to say. It was hard to tell when he was being serious or when he was joking. He was a sarcastic man; tall with broad shoulders. He looked a bit intimidating, but to her, he was just a teddy bear. He provided a soft and calm place for her to be. His patience was something she loved the most about him. He was always full of life, working hard, chipper in spirit, and always on the go. He had a calm, happy go lucky demeanor and a loving heart. Losing him was the hardest thing she ever experienced. It still plagued her to this day.

Addison's parents had a deep connection; a love that captured the room with its lighthearted nature and sincere desire and awareness for one another. They were inseparable. Seeing her mom go through such a loss made it difficult. For a long time, moving forward was near impossible. There were months where Addison took care of herself. Her mom couldn't physically do it. Close friends would stop by and take the load off her mother, but it wasn't the same. Addison wanted her mom. She was hurting too. She was on the threshold of adulthood, and she didn't know how to cope with such devastation. As much as she wanted to tell her mom to get out of bed and be present, deep down, she knew her mom just didn't know what to do without him, and she was heartbroken and depressed. He was the strength of their family unit. He was the protector. It took a good year and a half before Addison really saw her mom come back to life. It happened in little increments. She slowly came out of her room more and more. She began going outside and gardening again. She visited her friends; she went back to work; she started laughing again. It made Addison happy to feel joy in the house after such a horrific event.

As sad as it was to lose her dad, this had to be worse. Addison's mom was the last real family member she had. Her mom was the one person she looked up to, the one person that supported her through anything and everything. It was unbearable to think of a life without her, and that only made the regret and guilt worse. Addison took her shirt sleeve and wiped her eyes. Trying to collect her thoughts, straightening her clothes and controlling her emotions, she reset her thinking, bringing her back to the present moment. It was time to do what she came for. It was time to head out and go to town. Addison needed to see what awaited her at her mom's antique store. She needed to gage the amount of time and work it would require to clean everything up and put it on the market for sale.

The antique store, alone, carried so many memories, Addison felt conflicted. She had been going back and forth on it. Should she sell it, or shouldn't she? Would her mom want her to keep it? Every time she thought about it, it made her wince. She didn't want to run a store, nor did she expect to stay in Edgerton. She was anticipating closing the shop and getting back to New York as fast as possible. Edgerton and New York City were night and day. They were opposite lifestyles. One was quiet and quaint, and the other was loud and busy. She didn't get to talk it over with her mom, so it felt unresolved. Would her mom be upset, knowing she didn't want to inherit her store and follow in her footsteps? Addison wondered if her mind would change once she saw it. Only time would tell. Leaving her mother's bedroom and heading down the stairs, Addison grabbed her things and left.

Chapter 3: Antiques

The brisk, foggy air was met with a mildewy frost that covered the ground and trees. Addison pulled her scarf in closer to her face, trying to block the breeze. She swiped her hands together, back and forth, to create heat and then put them in her pockets as she walked the streets. There was an old-fashioned attractiveness to Edgerton; it was picturesque in the way that every house and building lined up. The rooflines, the trim, the coloring, the curb appeal, classic and cottage-like. It felt welcoming and warm. Everything was different, yet it was just the same. A few new storefronts, new landscaping, and updated roadways and walkways had appeared, but otherwise, it had the same feel. It felt weird to be there. Addison was anticipating the nerves billowing up in her body as she got closer to her mom's antique store. The store was the pride and joy of their family, a business that had been in place since 1930. It had been passed down from generation to generation. Many times, in the midst of bad financial times, it almost switched hands. But by the grace and grit of faith and hard work, something always came through. The store had a familiar, home-like atmosphere that drew people in, making it a town treasure. The pressure of what to do with it plagued Addison's heart. She didn't want to take care of it. This wasn't her life anymore, but the stress of closing down a company with so much history felt wrong.

A few friendly faces waved at her to say hello; cheery and delightful as they passed her on the street. She waved politely. Taking notice of their demeanor, Addison couldn't help but think how different this town was compared to her life in New York. No one in New York waved at each other just for the pure kindness of it. As she kept walking, she could see the awning of the store as she came up to Main Street. It hadn't changed a bit. A smile came across her face.

As she reached the sidewalk and stood right in front of the window, she took in the exterior. Red and black bricks with blue painted trim and two dormer windows, decorated with white lights. It was so charming. Her mother had quite the eye and knew how to put things together just so. It felt warm, welcoming, and inviting. Maybe that was because it was like her second home when she was little, and it was bringing back fond memories. She had spent so many nights and weekends there. Nonetheless, it made her happy as they played out in her head. Distressed cupboards and buckets, crocks of all sizes, woven wicker and splint oak baskets, a primitive and rustic 1920's old nailed bench in milk green paint, and a vintage child's chair filled the window-scape. Addison marveled at the chair. She could hear her mom's voice explaining its origin. "It's from the Louis Phillippe time period, dating back to 1840. It's French. It's marvelous, Addy. Look at the details; the backrest and base were made in a chain of balls. The seat made of interwoven burlap. It's special, my darling, just like you." Her mother could find beauty in anything. She believed in every item's rarity, that no two things were the same, and each thing possessed a past and history meant to be shared. Addison had a picture of herself as a young five-year-old girl sitting in that chair with her favorite stuffed bunny and blanket.

Maybe I should keep the chair, she thought.

A wreath of magnolia hung from a piece of burlap upon the door. She touched it ever so slightly, fixing its position and straightening it. Snow and debris were collecting on the ground near the entrance. She took her foot and swiped the dirt away, to push it to the side and clear a walkway. Next to the door, a galvanized metal post box was attached to the siding. Addison stepped closer to open it and check the mail. She pulled out a stack of envelopes. As she rifled through them, she noticed bill after bill. *"Ugh,"* she huffed. The finances were another issue, something she didn't know enough about and didn't want to be in control of. That was one of the main reasons she couldn't wait to get it sold. She wanted the lawyer and accountant to work it all out.

Turning back towards the door, she placed the key in the knob, turning it to unlock it. But it wouldn't budge. Trying to get in, she wiggled the knob and pushed slightly on its weight to maneuver its position, but it was jammed. With force, she pushed harder, loosening it from the seal. As the door came loose, she fell forward, stumbling into the store. The loud ding-a-ling of bells echoed in the room as she entered. Walking in, a fragrance so familiar to her came over her at once, bringing her straight into the holiday mood. It felt like Christmas. A waft of cinnamon, spice, and apple instantly filled her with emotion, triggering a sense of melancholy and comfort from when she used to visit and help her mom in the store. They had the grandest time decorating the tree with tinsel and ornaments. She felt partly happy, partly sad. Mourning her mother would be something she had to get used to. Deep down inside, she felt as if her mom was going to show up at any moment, that she would walk through the doors in her normal, cheery fashion.

Looking around at all the collectibles, she marveled at them. She used to think it was all junk, and it had no meaning. But now, it was just the opposite. Everything in some way meant something. Each object represented a part of her mom's unique, intrinsic style. The keepsakes were treasures and mementos that she found while rummaging stores and markets all across the state. Things Addison often saw as trash, her mom found importance and meaning in.

Addison walked around, contemplating her options on what to do with everything... *Garage sale, donations, online store, auction ...*

Picking things up, looking over their worn appearance, she knew it was going to be hard to part with them. The only way she could let them go was if they went with someone who loved antiques as much as her mom. As she walked to the front of the store, she stopped and looked at a few pieces of art. *Hmm ... different.* A few canvases of abstract drawings rested upon the wall. It was a series. One was the outline of a woman. The second was a man and a woman meeting. In the third, it was love ... passionate, in your face, love. Full of color. Full of beauty and emotion. Next to the canvases lay a stack of illustration books, some old sketches, used art supplies, and different sized vases and glassware. Even though most of it was used, they didn't look vintage or primitive. Interested in the artist, she looked at the bottom of the paintings to see a signature. JB were the initials in the corner. She pulled out her phone and wrote them down, so she could research it. Continuing to scan all the items one time over, she went to the entryway, once more, and placed her hand on the store sign. She felt each letter under

32

her fingertip--- M-o-n-a-'s. Her mom had it custom-made. The store felt like her, charming and eclectic, with a homey and warm essence.

This is going to be harder than I thought. How can I close this? She is wrapped up in every item that inhabits this place.

Taking off her jacket, Addison went behind the counter and set her stuff down. She found little notes, reminders, purchase orders, receipts, and a calendar sitting by the register. Sighing, full of emotion, she took in her mom's handwriting. She opened the calendar and looked through it. Some of it had initials and codes for things, but other things were simple, like birthdays and special occasions. Addison turned to the month of May and saw her name on the fifteenth with a smiley face and cake sticker. Her mom never forgot anything. She made everyone feel special and important and always bought the most sentimental, personal gifts. Some would say she was nearly perfect.

Random townsfolk walked by the shop window with a wave. Addison didn't know who they were, but she was amused with their kind nature and waved back. It was going to take some getting used to. She wasn't sure how much waving and cheerfulness she could handle at the moment. As she looked over the shop, she could tell no one had been maintaining it for some time, it was covered in dust. Her incessant need to keep things tidy took over. Taking a broom that was hanging on a hook in the corner, she started to sweep. In order to begin the cleaning process, she did what her mom would have done, a good once over on the floors. Making piles, she got down low and brushed it into her dust pan.

The door swung open, and the ringing of the bells echoed across the shop.

Addison got up off the floor, sweeping the dust from her knees.

"Hello, how can I help you?"

"Addison, darling, hello. I'm so glad it is you. I got scared for a minute. I saw the shop open, and I couldn't believe it. For a moment, I thought maybe someone had bought it. Every time I go by lately, I think of Mona."

Addison started to get choked up. "Oh, Mrs. Walters, I'm so happy to see you." Her voice was shaky and meek. "I'm sorry for getting emotional; I am just overwhelmed being back here."

"I know, sweetie. I know."

Mrs. Walters, while older and primarily a manageress of the town, was Mona's best friend. Some would say they were like sisters. She was like a second mom to Addison for most of her childhood.

Addison tried putting her feelings into words. "I … I thought it would be easier. Knowing she was sick. I thought preparing myself would ease the pain, but it hasn't. Being back here makes it feel real, and I can feel her absence in everything. It is not easy. I miss her."

Mrs. Walters got choked up. "Addison, your mother wouldn't want you to be so broken up; she would want you to think of only positive things and move forward. Have you thought about what to do with the house and the store?"

Addison looked around the store. "I hate saying it out loud, but I can't keep them. I live too far away. There's no way I can manage. I can't afford to keep them running on my own. It hurts me to say this, but I'm going to put them up for sale. I need to pack her things up and go through her boxes. If you want anything, please let me know."

"I can stop by and help you."

"I'd appreciate that."

"What are you doing for Christmas, dear?"

"I will still be here, probably alone, sitting with my hot chocolate around the fire, listening to Christmas music." Addison shrugged her shoulders and side smiled.

"Oh no, dear. I could never let that happen. You can come spend the holiday with us. We are having some family and close friends over. We would love for you to join us. Mona would be so angry with me if she knew I didn't have you over. You can't spend Christmas alone. It's about family and love. You need people around you."

"All right. I will think about it, thanks."

"You should come to the Holiday Festival tonight. It is going to be amazing. My granddaughter is in the parade. Come see her. She would love another fan. She loved your mother, and it would be nice if she could put a face with the name. Mona spoke about you all the time to everyone."

"I'm sure she did." Addison tried holding back her tears.

"Only because she loved you very much and was so proud of you."

"I know. She was the best." Addison started to break down again.

"I didn't mean to upset you, darling."

Addison wiped her face and took a few deep breaths in. She got herself under control. "What time is the festival?"

"Six o'clock. It will be a full winter affair. There will be all sorts of things going on. You will probably see people you haven't been in touch with in a long time."

Yep. That's what I'm afraid of, Addison thought. "I'll try. I will see how long it takes me to get through all of this. I have a lot to finish up."

"Okay then, I will leave you to it. See you soon, sweetie." Mrs. Walters headed towards the door but then stopped and turned around. "You know, you look just like her; you have always had her beautiful smile. Keep it going, Addy. Be happy. Honor her memory."

Addison nodded kindly. "Will do. Bye, Mrs. Walters."

"After all these years, you can call me Wanda." She winked at Addison.

Addison smiled. "Okay, Aunt Wanda."

Wanda laughed, and her face softened hearing those words. "Do you remember calling me that as a little girl?"

"I do. I'm not sure why I ever stopped. When did I get so official?"

They both laughed.

"I think it was in your teenage years. You were independent and strong-willed. You wanted people to take you seriously, and you didn't want everyone to know we were as close as we were, since I was the town librarian. You wanted to call me what everyone else did, so it didn't draw attention. And I couldn't blame you. Kids can be mean. Anyway, dear, I loved you, nonetheless, and I still do. You are still my little Addy Cakes. I'm glad you are here for a while. Your face, it lights this place up. It's a delight."

Addison blushed. "Thank you for stopping in."

Addison went up to Wanda and gave her a hug, embracing her with love.

Wanda let go and went to the door. "I'm going down to the confectionary to enjoy the gingersnaps that Bob Costello made. You have got to try them. They are a delectable treat. They will for sure make you feel a little better. Or at least keep your belly full."

"Yum. Thanks for the recommendation. I'll stop there on my way out." Addison smiled and waved goodbye.

Returning to her cleaning and taking brown cardboard boxes out from the backroom to start organizing, Addison started sorting breakables and glassware. She created three piles: donations, collectibles, and sales items. Something kept plaguing her. How could she make the decision on what went in what box? What if she threw something in the donation pile, but it was a collectible? She knew nothing about antiques. This was her biggest fear, getting rid of things that meant something to someone.

Just then, the old, faded sleigh bells rang once again, getting Addison's attention.

She turned towards the door.

"Hello," Addison said cheerfully.

"Oh, hi," a gentleman answered back, alarmed by her greeting, not seeing her there. He had his sights on something near the window.

"Can I help you?" she asked.

"I'm just looking."

"We are not really open. Sorry. I know it's a bit confusing, because I'm in here, the lights are on, and the door is open, but I'm actually packing things up. The store is being sold."

"Oh, you are kidding? I'm sorry to hear that. Are you Mona?"

"No. I am her daughter, Addison."

"Sorry. I just figured since you were in here."

"That's okay. How do you know of my mother's name?"

"Not to state the obvious or anything, but the name of the store is Mona's."

Addison started laughing. "Touché."

"Do you work here too?" he questioned.

"No. I don't. I'm just here for the holidays. Are you a regular? Do you live around here?"

"No, I'm just visiting my dad. He hasn't been himself lately, so I thought I'd stay for a few days until he's back on his feet. He lives outside of town. I don't live far either, just a few towns over, about forty-five minutes west of here."

"Nice. What brought you into town today?"

"I told him I'd go out for a little bit and bring back dinner, but he didn't seem interested or have much of an appetite. Basically, he wanted me to leave. So, I figured I'd check out the parade, since I didn't have much else to do. I'm just wandering around until then."

Addison chuckled. "Parents ... they are stubborn, aren't they?"

"You are telling me. My dad might be the most stubborn man I know."

"I think as they get older they don't want to lose who they are, and they just want to do it their way, the way they've done it their whole life."

"Sounds like you know a little bit about that."

"Yeah, my mom was sick for a while. I tried helping her, but she wouldn't let me in much. She was set in her own ways. She didn't want to bother me and wanted to show everyone that she was capable and useful, regardless of what she was going through. I think she always prided herself on being a strong woman. She didn't want anyone to think less of her. Sorry, I don't know why I'm talking about this with you. I just met you."

"Don't be sorry. I get it. My dad is still sharp-witted and independent. He really likes his alone time. But there's something to it lately that alarms me. He just seems sad. Maybe its loneliness. I just don't like knowing that he's out there, in the country by himself.

Addison nodded her head but didn't respond, making Jack feel vulnerable.

"Now look at me. I'm the one rambling," he said.

"Sorry, I was just thinking as you were talking. You know … sometimes, we have to give them that space and allow them to open up when they feel comfortable. Or we have to make a better effort in doing it, even if they say no. But you already know that. If I could go back, I would have imposed myself on my mom a little more. I don't know if that is more for me or more for her, but I regret not trying harder in the moment."

He looked like he wanted to change the subject. "So, you grew up here in Edgerton, I'm assuming?" he asked.

"Yes. It's pretty strange being back here. You?"

"No. I grew up in Waterford. I still live there. My dad moved here some time ago, after my mom passed. He needed a change of scenery."

"Perfect town to come to. Sorry about your mom."

The gentleman nodded his head in acknowledgment and kept picking up small objects, looking at the bottoms.

Addison began to pry further. "Are you in the antique business? You seem to be looking for something specific."

"No. I just remembered that my dad mentioned donating a few things awhile back, and I was just peeking in to see if they were still around,

40

if I could find them. I figured it would be a stretch. I thought maybe if I found something, and I brought it back to him, it would lift his spirits. They were family mementos, if you will. At the time, he gave them away because he didn't want to hold on to the memory and sadness, but now, I think maybe it would cheer him up. I don't know. Maybe it wouldn't. I just thought it was worth a try. But I'm not even sure exactly how many he gave away or how many times he donated. He just mentioned this store quite a bit."

"I wonder if he knew my mom?" Addison waited for him to respond, but he didn't. "Well, if you tell me what they are, I can look for them."

"One was from World War II; it had an inscription on it. It is called an entrenching tool. And the other one is a scraper, used for tools. It had a vintage wood handle. I'm sure they were sold."

Addison started walking around the store. "It might take me awhile to look through everything. Do you want to leave your number? I can call you if I find them."

"Sure. That would be great. I'm Jack." He walked up to the counter by the register and wrote down his number on a notepad that was lying there.

"Okay, Jack. Nice to meet you."

"You too, Addison."

They smiled cordially at one another with a hint of flirtation.

Addison eyed the number on the paper. "An 860-area code, huh? Is that un-incorporated?"

"Yes, that must be what they give people when they decide to stay away from civilization. It's my dad's. I figured a land line would be your best bet on getting through. My cell phone doesn't have good service. Just make sure you ask for me, so he doesn't catch on that I'm looking for this stuff." He chuckled.

Addison laughed. "Okay, will do. I bet the countryside is nice and peaceful to wake up to," Addison professed. "Sometimes, I crave quietness, away from it all."

"Ten acres of rolling hills. It's a horse farm."

"Wow. Sounds heavenly. Most of my mornings, I wake up to drilling, the honking of cars, yelling, and other wonderful city sounds. I could use a little bit of serenity these days. That's something I haven't had in quite some time. Being back here will be nice for my sanity."

"You live in the city?"

Addison shook her head yes. "New York."

"Definitely different than here. What made you choose the city life over Edgerton? I am just curious."

"At the time, I just wanted a fresh, clean break. I was ready to experience something new and exciting. I wanted the challenge, energy, and diversity of a big city. I've always wanted to make it big in the business world. I knew that wouldn't happen here."

"I see. I'm glad you are happy there."

"Lately, I have been questioning it, if I am honest."

"I do the same thing from time to time. But then, I go back to my roots, and I remember what makes me, me."

"That's a good way of looking at it."

"Stop out by my dad's sometime, while I'm here. Come to the farm. I'll show you what I'm talking about."

Addison was thrown that he was so inviting and forward. She didn't know what to say in return. Was he serious? How was it that they could have such a deep conversation and an immediate connection, within moments of meeting? She started to put her walls up and close herself off. She could feel herself pulling back. She played coy, tossing her chocolate brown, auburn hinted hair and pulling her fingers through the ends.

"As for those artifacts, hopefully I will find them in the next day or so. There's so much to do, so many things to sift through. I'm a little overwhelmed. No one tells you about the after effects of a parent's death when you are the executor of the estate. Beyond the loss itself, figuring out what to do with all their stuff is a job all of its own," she said.

Jack closed his eyes, took a deep breath, and sighed. "I didn't realize ..."

"That's okay. How would you?"

"Your mom or your dad?" he asked, interested.

"Mom. Mona." Addison pointed to the storefront that had the name imprinted on it.

"Ah ... I see. So, you are selling the shop because she's gone? Was it recent?" A distressed look came over his face. He looked defeated or confused. She couldn't place it, but he immediately went into a different head space.

"Two weeks ago. And I don't have the means to keep it open. I don't live close enough to stop in all the time, and I don't know enough about this type of business."

"Well, I'm sorry for your loss. I take it your dad isn't around then?"

"He died when I was younger. It's been us two for quite some time now."

"Gosh, I'm sorry. That has to be difficult."

"It's a weird feeling knowing that both of your parents are gone."

"I haven't felt that loss yet, but when my mom passed, my dad didn't know what to do with himself. He didn't know how to run the household. He was used to having everything done for him. She cooked, cleaned, did the shopping, the bills, the scheduling. When she died, a part of him died too."

"You know, if anyone knows what you are talking about, I definitely do. I can relate to everything you just said. Losing a parent is hard enough but watching the other one mourn the other is even worse. I tried telling my mom that I needed her after my dad passed, but many days, for a long time, she just couldn't muster the strength or energy to get out of bed. He took

44

care of us; he was the breadwinner; he kept us safe. She had to find herself again and start anew. It took a long time."

Jack took her in with his eyes, noticing her natural beauty. He was a bit overwhelmed with how she made him feel. "Look at us, going on and on."

Addison could feel him staring, and she liked it. "I know, so depressing, I'm sorry."

"Please quit saying I'm sorry."

"Okay. Sor ..." Addison caught herself and then closed her eyes and smiled.

Jack slightly laughed seeing her catch herself. "I'm sure your mom was a very special lady."

"Thank you. That means a lot. She was always energetic and magnetic in personality. A little quirky at times, but I think that's what I loved about her. She made me laugh. I will miss her for sure." Addison looked down and tried choking back her sorrow.

"I didn't mean to upset you." Jack leaned towards her, grabbing a tissue from the counter, handing her one.

"No, I'm being overly sensitive today. It's a fresh wound. Coming here turned me into a pile of mush. It is the first time in a long time that I'm seeing her things."

Addison turned around and tried calming herself down. She was embarrassed.

Jack didn't want to overwhelm her anymore, so he started walking around the store. He scanned a few more knick-knacks that rested on a sales table that were out for display and kept looking at the art stuff. "It's crazy how many collectibles and artifacts there are, that have traveled year to year, place to place, that were a part of one's life at some point. Each thing has a story. Or so they say."

"That sounds like something my mom would have said. She was passionate about antiques. She believed there was a purpose for everything. The looks on her customers' faces gave her such happiness when they found something meaningful. I never truly understood it until now. Gosh, it's like de ja vu hearing you say that. I can't believe it."

Jack picked up a red, 19th century Tole Tabac trade sign, also known as a carrot due to its rounded and tapered shape. Attached was a small description of its origin. It was from France, where they used it in a tobacco shop. It was hand beaten in three different sections and then shaped into one. The carrot was supported with a simple iron hook to be wall mounted. A set of playing cards, cups, and crossed smoking pipe motifs was hand painted on the exterior of the cylindrical piece. It had crackled paint with the remains of gold gilt paint across the center sections; aged patina with weathering, fading, and scratches. He looked it over. "My dad would like this. He has a house full of antiques. Not that he needs any more, but it might make him feel good."

"Go ahead and take it."

"I'll pay you for it. It's probably expensive."

"No, really, please take it."

"Well, that's awfully nice of you. Thank you. You know, it looks like you could use a break. Would you like to go to the festival? I'm just about to head there."

Addison took a breath and dropped her shoulders, realizing just how high and tense they were. She wasn't sure she was up for such a thing, but she loved that he asked her. She was flattered. "I keep hearing about this festival and parade. We used to have something similar when I was a kid, but on a much smaller level. It gets bigger every year, I hear. The baking competitions, the lighting of the tree, the storefronts, everyone tries to out-do each other. My mom used to get so involved. She lived for this time of year."

Jack smiled. "Then you should definitely see it, if you haven't been to one since your childhood. Come see how things have changed."

"I'm not sure."

"C'mon, I could use a friendly face to join me. I'll buy you something from the sweet shoppe. You look like you could use a getaway for a while. They have all sorts of Christmas confectionaries to enjoy. Large hot chocolates with big candy canes and marshmallows, giant sugar cookies and freshly made fudge. Does any of that interest you?"

Smiling, Addison put her hand on her stomach. "Okay. I could use a break. I do have a sweet tooth. And my stomach has been growling. I will come back another day and do this. I could use a friendly face just as much as you. Also, I heard the gingersnaps are out of this world."

As Addison locked up the back door, shut the register, and grabbed her coat and scarf, she noticed him fixated on something. Back to the front window, he lingered near the painting of the man and woman in love. It was the same thing he looked at when he first walked in.

"Are you sure you haven't been in here before?" Addison asked.

"I'm sure."

"I thought maybe you had. It's just … you seem interested in that piece. I figured maybe you had seen it before. Do you know the artist? I saw it earlier today. There was no signature, but there are initials in the corner. It's so different than what my mom usually has in here. You seem attached and drawn to it for some reason."

"It just reminds me of someone; it's so vaguely familiar to me. There's something about it that I've seen before, the way its constructed, the drawing, the lines, the colors, I can't put my finger on it exactly."

Jack stared at the corner and placed his finger over the initials, JB. Jack's mannerisms and body language made Addison curious, as he gazed at it. She could tell he was drawn to it, or it was sparking something within him.

"Anything sparking your memory?" she asked.

"MM … I'm not sure."

"I want you to have it. It's yours."

"Oh, no, no, no. You don't have to do that. You don't even know who the artist is. What if it's an expensive piece? What if it meant something to your mom? I just couldn't."

"No, seriously. Please. I would like it to go to someone that has appreciation for it."

"Well, if you are sure. But don't hunt me down if it's an original Monet or something like that."

"I promise you, I won't. I am sure."

"Thank you. I'll grab it another day, if that's okay? So, I don't have to carry it around the festival."

"Yeah, that would be fine. Maybe your dad would enjoy taking a visit to the shop, since I'm getting rid of everything. I would love for another antique lover to have some of these things or give me advice on what to keep."

Jack ignored her comment. He headed towards the door, opened it, and stepped out. "You ready to go see what this festival is all about?"

Addison walked forward and looked into his green eyes, while adoring his dimples and the inset of his chin. "Yes. I'm ready."

His sandy colored hair, a little curly in the back, gelled and combed to the side, outlined his oval face and accentuated the features of his small eyes and friendly smile, leaving Addison a bit mesmerized. He was her type. Clean cut with an organic nature to him that let off a down to earth, loyal vibe. There was a humility in his voice and honesty in his eyes. He exuded a kind heart, and it made Addison feel nervous in his presence. His tall and toned stature was appealing. His personality was nothing close to ordinary, and it was completely and utterly refreshing. She hadn't met someone so real and authentic in who they were in such a long time.

Addison started to lock the door, touching the silver bells that were upon it, unique and rare, and then looked over at Jack. "You see these sleigh bells ... I can't believe my mom kept them all these years. I know it's silly, but I got these when I was a small girl. I made a Christmas wish, and they showed up under the tree in a small box with my present. They brought me a lot of good luck through the years. When she took over for my grandma, I gave them to her, and she put them on the door and said they would bring good luck to anyone that walked in."

"Then, I think you should hang on to those. You can always use good luck," said Jack.

"And since you walked in today, I assume that includes you," Addison said flirtatiously.

He smiled. "This might sound forward or cringeworthy, but I can't remember the last time ..." Jack took a second to compose his thought. Her eyes staring into his made him flush, turning his cheeks red. "Okay, let me get this straight, because I want to say it correctly ... It's just ... I can't remember the last time I saw a person with as much natural beauty as you have. I know that sounds like a line, but it's true. I can't help it. I'm going to give you compliments. That's who I am."

Blushing and completely taken with his compliment, Addison giggled. "No."

"Yeah, you have blown me away a bit, I'm not going to lie."

They looked at each other with intention in their eyes, feeling smitten with one another.

Addison finished locking up, and they began walking down the street, taking in the scene. Jack pulled on her jacket slightly, keeping her close to his side, so they didn't get separated by the crowd of people. She was pleasantly surprised by his natural instinct and protective nature toward her.

Walking down the sidewalk, trying to move forward, past everyone, Addison was amazed at the outpouring. "Wow. You weren't kidding. It sure has grown. Yet, it still feels the same. There aren't many towns like this, with so much Christmas magic and spirit. I used to walk this exact street with my parents, one hand in each of theirs, feeling like anything could be. It's like a real 'live' snow globe scene."

Jack looked at her, wanting to assure her that it was still possible to feel such happiness. "It can still be that way."

She looked at him, and their eyes met, creating a moment of romantic connection. Addison blushed but ignored his kind sentiments, giving no response. Was he for real? She had never met a man of his caliber. He seemed too good to be true.

Jack interrupted the moment. "Look at all the carolers."

"It's amazing. You would think this was a set for a movie or something."

"Enjoy it. Look around. Take it in."

Addison scanned the crowd. So many people surrounded them, full of high-energy, exuding a jolly spirit. So much Christmas cheer. It was nostalgic. It was as if everything was perfectly placed and set. A smile burst across Addison's face, and a child-like euphoria came over her. Jack admired her experience, seeing her feeling sprightly for the first time. He marveled at the dewy, soft nature of her pale skin, as the moonlight hit it just so; so smooth and refined. He thought she was beautiful. It took everything in him to not be obvious and direct about it. He adored the freckles that covered the top of her nose and under her eyes. Her dark hair and her blue eyes, they were captivating. Most of all, he was enamored by her full smile, full of wonder and ethereal beauty, outlining her glowing cheekbones and petite features. Her blushed cheeks, her soft pink lips … they were perfect to him. He was interested in her and wanted to get to know her better. How could she feel so much like home? And why did she feel so disconnected from her roots that she was so far away in the big city?

Jack didn't want to interrupt her moment of happiness, but he wanted to add substance to their conversation. It wasn't often that he had such a connection with someone, let alone a stranger. He began to pry. "What do you do for a living, by the way? What took you to that big city, away from here?"

Addison smiled and then shrugged her shoulders. "Honestly, I ask myself the same question sometimes. What is it that I really do? I am a jack of all trades, I can say that. Job title wise, I'm an account executive at Doxens. Not too much to brag about just yet, but I'm working my way up. It's a good company. I basically do the grunt work. Initially, I went to NYU to earn my bachelor's degree. I never came back. I don't know if that was a good decision or a bad decision. Since Mom passed, I have been thinking it might have been a bad decision. But I can't dwell on the what ifs and the negatives, because they will swallow me up. How about you?"

Jack nodded his head, listening intently to her words. "You have to start somewhere, right?"

Addison agreed. "Yep. At least that is what I tell myself."

Jack smiled. "To answer your question, I work with animals, one of my favorite things."

"Mine too, go figure. Can you elaborate? Like, what kind of animals?" Addison asked.

"Mainly farm animals. Lots of cows. I'm a vet. They call me The Animal Dr."

"That's impressive. Do I have to call you that?"

"You can call me whatever you want."

Addison was so amused by him and his candor, and she was highly impressed by his job. She began to look him over, taking him in with her eyes. "You know, some would say we are matching under our coats. I didn't even notice that earlier."

They looked at each other, up and down. Jack cocked his head. "Cute. I'm not sure I would have noticed that if you hadn't pointed it out."

"I have to say, you look better. You pull off the flannel look effortlessly."

"You have that whole winter casual vibe going for you."

"Fancy by day, casual by night," Addison said while laughing.

"You have this confidence about you, yet you seem so laid-back."

"My mom used to tell me that was one of my best traits when finding a man. I adapt, and I am low-maintenance."

"Do you date or go out often?"

"Not really. You?"

"Here and there. Nothing serious. What would you say is your normal type?"

Addison looked at him. "Someone with a sense of humor, someone who is relatively tall. I wouldn't mind if he was easy on the eyes … good physique, light colored hair, good style."

Jack, amused, glanced at her and side smiled. "Mmm … I see."

"How about you?" Addison asked, feeling extremely vulnerable.

"Nice skin, good teeth, dark hair, someone that takes good care of themselves."

"We seem like quite the pair right now with all our similarities and likes. Maybe it's because we are twinning. Team plaid all the way," Addison joked.

They both laughed. They were amused with each other and the easy flow of the conversation.

"Yep, we set the vibe. If we do it again the next time I see you, we may have to discuss pre-arranging our outfits, so we don't look like dorks," Jack said.

"Well, I think it's kind of cute." Addison was delighted hearing him mention the idea of seeing her again.

"Yeah, if we are taking a family photo or something, but if I want to stay original and up my fashion game, I'm not sure that's the way to do it." He laughed.

"You got me there." Addison bit her bottom lip. She was enjoying his company and felt an electricity between them that she couldn't figure out. They had just met, but it felt like the most real connection she had ever experienced. They definitely had chemistry. She just couldn't pinpoint what made it feel so unique and special. He made her feel safe and comforted, and there was a warmth that emanated off of him. His energy was calming but alluring. It had been a long time since she was with a real man, not a pretentious man-boy. He had his stuff together; he seemed to know who he was, and from what she could gather, he led with his heart. Being in his presence made her feel wholesome and lighthearted. It was friendly yet exciting. She wanted to keep the banter going. "So, wearing matching jean shirts is out of the question?" Addison slightly laughed to herself.

"Hmmm …" He drew in the left side of his face, scrunching his brows and squinting his eyes.

55

"That's what we wore for our last family photo shoot, so I figured I'd put it out there," Addison said.

Jack chuckled, trying to imagine it. "I'd like to see those photos."

"Ha. Never."

"Now that you told me, you can't deprive me of such greatness."

"I know. It was a full family affair. Aunts, uncles, cousins. Enough denim for a lifetime."

"Jean on jean, I am assuming?"

"Yep."

"Well, that's not as bad as my family's ugly Christmas sweater photo. I'd like to burn that one."

"That sounds like fun. At least the intention was to be funny."

"Yep, and good old Jack, right here, was Santa Claus; beard, hat, belly, and all."

"I bet you made a great Santa Claus. Santa Jack or Dr. Santa has a good ring to it."

"I retired the costume. I'll let the real Santa have that job."

"I think you missed your calling."

Jack interrupted and motioned her to move to the side. "Let's stand over here. We will get a good view."

Addison followed him, pushing through the gathering of people, standing at the forefront of the town square. Every noise, every motion, and every smell hit Addison at once. She was entranced. The feelings of when she was a little girl came rushing back. The Christmas spirit enveloped her in its joyousness.

A giant fire burned in the center of the square. Guitarists played soft harmonies of "Jingle Bells" and "Joy to the World." Snowmen contests were set up along the fenced in lawn of the courthouse. Carolers sang "We Wish You a Merry Christmas," greeting patrons as they entered and exited each restaurant and store along the cobblestone walkway. Large gingerbread houses filled the window-scape of the corner bakery. Everything was glowing from hundreds of decorated lights. There were assorted colors, among silver ribbons that highlighted the scene. Street lamps lined the pathways of the village, making everything glisten. White lit snowflakes hung along a line of steel, dangling from above, sparkling over the walkways. A blow-up Santa Claus blew in the wind, his hat moving to and fro. A long line of kids waited next to the post office to visit Mrs. Claus, Santa, and the elves. Each took a picture, told their wishes in Santa's ear, and sent off their finalized letters to the North Pole.

Addison felt airy and light. Her eyes widened, looking at everything. "I just can't believe it's gotten this big. This is wonderful."

Jack's eyes grew wide too. "I know. It's pretty spectacular; there's not much like it. This town, in a sense, holds everything Christmas is about. Last year, the local news did a story on Edgerton. The town with all the Christmas magic, they called it. Like you said, it's like a storybook."

"Wow. I didn't know that. That's fantastic to hear. What a special treat for Edgerton. The townsfolk must have been so happy to get that recognition. I am surprised my mom didn't send me the article."

"Maybe she knew you were busy."

"I always took Edgerton for granted. As a kid, I wanted so badly to get out of here. I used to watch tv and see these big Christmas trees, surrounded by these big ice rinks, with tons of shopping and thousands of people from all over the world. They had these fancy coats and this luxurious lifestyle. I wanted to be a part of it, thinking it would fill me up. Once I got there, it was different. Surreal to say the least. It had everything I was searching for, but the feeling wasn't there. The tree lighting was nice, but it wasn't home. It wasn't with the people I loved; it didn't feel the same. If I'm honest, I felt a bit lonely. It was something I always wanted, but it wasn't what I expected. It's gotten better, the longer I've been there, but it's still a process, finding myself. I've never admitted that to anyone."

"Why haven't you?"

"I never wanted my mom to know that I struggled emotionally. She believed I was this self-sufficient city girl, taking it all on. I made it seem so great. She was so proud of me. What she didn't realize is that I missed her. I missed Edgerton. I missed this small-town vibe … this exact feeling that I'm feeling right now. I just wish I could have told her."

"She knows." Jack winked at her. Changing the topic, he pointed at a beverage cart that was passing in front of them. "Thirsty? They are giving away free cider."

"I would love some."

Jack took a few steps forward, grabbed two cups, and then handed one to Addison. "The parade is lining up; it's going to start any minute now. I hope all the children getting ready to sing in the parade aren't too cold. It's pretty brisk out here."

"I'm sure they are loving every minute. How can they not? This is the most wonderful time of the year."

"Someone is filled with Christmas joy."

"I guess this festival is bringing it out of me."

"Or I am..."

She looked over, trying to see his facial expression, but he played coy.

"You warm enough?" he asked.

"Yes, thanks."

"I would have given you my scarf."

Addison gasped, and her mouth dropped open. "Oh, man. I should have said yes. It's a nice one. You can't tempt me with good fashion." Addison pretended to reach over and grab it.

He chuckled and slightly pulled away, teasing her. "It's no longer up for grabs, since you said you are warm enough."

"Oh, it's mine now." Addison giggled, while slowly and playfully pulling it off of him. She put it around her neck and smiled.

Jack was amused. He smiled at her, finding her endearing. "I have to say, it looks perfect. It looks much better on you."

Addison's stomach was filled with butterflies. His energy was consuming. "You are a gentleman, and I appreciate that. Thank you."

Jack nodded his head, acknowledging her kind comment. Leaning over, he pulled Addison's hat down over her ears. "Even though you are warm, you don't want to catch a cold."

Addison smiled, straightened her hat, and tightened up her jacket buttons and collar. "Thank you, Dr."

The breath from each person in the crowd sifted in the air, creating puffs of white from the coldness. Everyone took their spots along the cobblestone streets, making sure they had a straight view, so they didn't miss anything. The parade started with retired military members playing the bagpipes, followed by the town sheriff, fire crew, and paramedic team. The mayor and town officials waved to everyone as they came through on horses that were adorned with Christmas wreaths and bells. The local school band played loudly to "Santa is Coming to Town." Large reindeer made of twigs and glitter lead the way on a big float for the dance team, who did a tumbling number to the beat of *The Nutcracker*. Toy soldiers marched, one by one, to the beat of drums. In the center of it all, was a large tree with a big red star on top. Behind it, came a bright red sleigh with Mr. & Mrs. Claus, dressed in hats and red cloaks. They had a large red sack that they were tossing candy canes out of. Standing up, they gave their best smile and wave, ending the night with a loud and joyful, "Ho, Ho, Ho."

As the parade came to an end, everyone began dispersing, talking to one other. Addison looked for anyone that she might know from her past, but no one stood out. Wanda came up behind her and tapped her on the shoulder.

"Addy, darling, I want you to meet someone."

Jack and Addison turned around and saw a little brunette girl with the rosiest of cheeks, dressed in all brown with an antler headband on, staring up at them. Addison bent over slightly and put her hand out.

"Well, hello. What is your name?"

"I'm Grace."

"You are the most beautiful reindeer I have ever seen, Grace."

Grace smiled big and showed her pearly white teeth, putting her hands up in front of her face, acting like paws.

"Grace, I am Addison. I hear you knew my mother, Mona."

"Yeah. She was really nice."

"Looks like you did a wonderful job in the parade. Did you have fun?"

"I did. I can't wait for Christmas day."

"I have a feeling you have been a really good girl, and you will have a great Christmas."

"I hope so."

"Did your grandma, here, bring you to the sweet shoppe yet?"

"No, not yet."

Wanda pulled money out of her purse and handed it to Grace. "Here, sweetie, go buy yourself a treat."

"Thank you, Grandma. Nice to meet you, Addison."

"You too, Grace. Hope to see you around."

Grace skipped off to be with her friends.

Wanda looked at Jack and then looked at Addison, jerking her head, hinting that she wanted an introduction.

Addison caught on. "Oh, Aunt Wanda, I'm sorry, this is my friend Jack. Jack, this was my mother's best friend, Wanda Walters."

Jack put his hand out to meet hers. "Wanda, it's a pleasure to meet you."

"You, too. How come I haven't seen you around before? Actually, you look vaguely familiar. Do you live in town?"

"No, I'm visiting my dad, James Beardsley. He hasn't been feeling well."

Wanda's eyes grew wide. "Oh, I'm sorry. Jack, I know your father. Please tell him hello for me. I wish him well."

"Thank you. I appreciate that. I will do that."

Wanda looked at Addison and then spoke quieter from the side of her mouth. "I didn't realize you knew each other?" Wanda pointed her finger back and forth between Jack and Addison.

"We just met today. He stopped in to see the shop," Addison said.

"He did? Jack were you looking for something specific?"

"Yeah, a few family heirlooms. I remembered my dad mentioning the store, so I popped in."

Wanda shook her head with a slight smile. "Well, how nice. And now you are out together." She gave Addison a wink. "I'm glad someone could get you out."

"We both needed a breather. I thought it would be nice to see the festival. Mom would be happy."

Wanda looked at Jack and Addison and shook her head yes. "Oh, yes, she would be. She is probably dancing in heaven right now. It's one of her favorite days of the year. I must say, it's almost as if she planned it herself. Maybe she's pulling the strings. Timing, it's a funny thing, huh? Well, I must go check on Grace. Nice to see you both. Have fun. Addy, I'll stop in soon."

Addison scrunched her forehead. *What did she mean by all that?* "Okay, see you soon, bye."

"Nice to meet you," Jack responded.

Addison looked at Jack. "That was kind of interesting, don't you think?"

"In what way?" he asked.

"I don't know. She just seemed to be rambling about us meeting."

"I just thought it was a cute aunt type of thing to do. She seemed happy that you were out with someone."

"Did it scare you off? Are you wishing you left me back at the antique store?" Addison smiled.

"No, I'm quite enjoying myself."

"Good. Me too."

They walked side by side, moving about the circle, people watching.

"Jack, did our parents know each other, you think? I think I asked you this earlier, but I don't recall you answering."

"They must have, seems like everyone knows everyone around here. And I assume if your Aunt Wanda did, then your Mom probably did, as well. My dad has ventured into her shop on occasion, so I'm sure they have struck up a conversation a time or two. Even though, now that I think about it, he isn't the most talkative man."

"Well, my mother was. She was a talker, a greeter, a cheerleader for humanity. She opened her arms to everyone, and it made you feel so good, so welcome. Maybe they were friends. You will have to mention it to your dad. Let me know what he says."

Jack looked elsewhere. "You know, I think I should probably get going. I need to check on the heater, sometimes it goes out. It's been finicky lately with the cold. He's probably sleeping, but I wouldn't feel good about myself if I didn't."

Addison stepped back, flustered, feeling like she took up too much of his time. "Oh, yeah, of course. Forgive me for taking up your time. Please, go. Do what you need to do. Don't stay because of me. I'm fine. I'm going to walk home and get in my pajamas. I need a good movie night." Unraveling the scarf from around her neck, she held it in her hand and put her arm out, giving it back to him.

Taking the scarf from her hand, Jack looked at her, charmed. "I'll be awaiting your call."

"My call?"

"You know … for the things in the shop that I was looking for."

Addison closed her eyes for a brief second and took a calming breath. *Of Course.* "That's right. Sorry, too much on my mind. I will definitely give you a call and let you know when or if I find them."

"Would you like me to walk you home?" he asked.

She hesitated and then looked around. "No. I'm good. I could use the time to myself. Thanks for offering."

"Sure. Have a good night."

"You too, Jack."

She turned and started walking the other way, towards her mom's house.

Jack called out to her. "Addison."

Turning her head to meet his voice, "Yes?"

"Matching jean shirts ... I can do that." He kept a smug smirk about his face.

Addison began giggling, blushing. "I'll be sure to find mine."

Jack put his hands in his pockets and looked directly in her eyes. "It was a good night."

She nodded yes and paused for a second. "Yeah. It was."

Smiling, Addison turned back around and kept walking home. She took in the smell of the pine trees and fresh snow. The sparkling, iridescent nature of the snowflakes, mirrored walkways of ice, and all the twinkling lights above made her feel transcendent. As the noise started to fade, getting further away from town, and she was alone again, she had to deal with the underlying sadness and pain that were there to greet her. It felt nice to have a distraction and a sense of comfort and companionship for a while. The silence, at times, was crippling.

Addison waved at the neighbors as she walked up the sidewalk to go into the house. She didn't want to talk to anyone. Holding a full conversation right now seemed grueling. She shut the door behind her and exhaled, letting every ounce of energy escape her. "Phew, time for bed," she said aloud. Placing her jacket on the coat rack, she took off her shoes and went upstairs to her bedroom. Her legs felt heavy and sore. Her feet were throbbing. She closed the bedroom door behind her to create a sense of safety and privacy. Changing into her pajamas and hopping into bed, she pulled the covers over her legs and fluffed her pillows. She turned on the television, letting the loud voices overtake the room. Exhaustion came over her. She could barely function; she was depleted of everything. Grabbing her purse on the floor by the bed, she pulled out the piece of paper with Jack's name on it. It made her smile. She placed it on her nightstand. Part of her thought about calling him. Something inside of her yearned to see him again. Addison knew that she couldn't. She needed to leave things as they were and trust that everything would play out in its own time.

Chapter 4: Loose Ends

It had been a few days of frigidly cold temperatures. Addison didn't leave the house much, except to go to the antique store. It had been snowing off and on. While she was in the store, she kept it locked up, so she couldn't be distracted by visitors. She consumed herself with getting things straightened out, spending hour after hour packing, sorting, and cleaning. She had mostly everything into their prospective piles and began calling nearby re-sale shops to find some of the more popular pieces new homes. She had one distinct pile for the unknowns. She wasn't sure what pile they belonged in, and she didn't know their importance, so she was afraid to give them away. She went over to the counter and wrote out a reminder for herself: *Call an appraiser.* As the days went by, it was starting to sink in that the shop was no longer in working order. It was bare bones with the addition of stacked boxes. It was still filled with warmth and memories, but it was losing its charm and appeal. She had mixed feelings. She was happy that she had accomplished so much but saddened by its emptiness. The details, the decorations, the love, the smell ... they were disappearing as the items did. There was a sense of anxiety billowing up inside her, knowing that upon completion, it would be the end of an era, and their family business would no longer exist. She wasn't sure if she was ready to say a final goodbye yet. Would she ever step foot in Edgerton again? She didn't really have a reason to come back. The thought created a somber feeling in her soul. Walking around the store, Addison went towards the window and looked out towards the street. She took in the simple things: the slight laughter of two friends talking while drinking coffee together, the walking of a dog, the energy of little ones skipping and jumping around under the dull, sunless sky, watching a family hold hands while walking through the park upon the stiff, frozen grass, the gentle breeze blowing a flag ever so slightly, and the simple movements of a simple life. The small-town quaintness was filling her with a sense of peace, something she hadn't felt in a long time.

After reveling in Edgerton's character, Addison took her sights back to the boxes. As she walked around, making sure the labels were correct, she grabbed a few boxes that were sitting in the corner and moved them over by the doorway, away from everything else. They were filled with things she'd saved for herself: things she couldn't part with, things she felt had memories attached to them, and mementos that reminded her of her mom. A truck had been stopping daily to pick up donations and garbage, and she heard it pull up. It was like clockwork at three o'clock every afternoon. She could hear the screeching of the tires as they put on the breaks; she could hear the doors close as the drivers got out; she could hear the loud, rattling, fluttering sound of the back-trailer door as they raised it open, and she heard the sounds of their footsteps coming towards the back. Every day, it was a reminder that nothing was staying. It was all leaving, and everything was changing. Addison unlocked the back door so they could come in. Two older gentlemen knocked before walking in.

"Come on in," Addison said with a smile.

"Hi, Ma'am. How are you doing today?" asked one of the men.

"I'm good, thank you. Looks like this is your last load to pick up. I can't believe it. Thanks for all your help."

"No problem."

"Would you like a cup of coffee or water for the road? I can grab you something?" Addison asked.

"No, we have to be on our way. We appreciate that though. Have a nice Christmas, and best of luck to you."

"You, as well."

As they continued to load the boxes, clearing everything out, she knew it was time to call in a real estate agent and officially put it up for sale. She waved goodbye to the gentlemen and locked the back door behind them.

Addison went to the cherry stained wood countertop where the phone was and dialed a number from a business card she had received in the mail. She dialed the number to Martha O'Riley from Edgerton Realty, someone her mother had known for years. The best real estate agent in the county. Martha was bubbly, boisterous, intrusive, demanding, and a bit over the top, but she was the right person for the job. She knew everyone in a fifty-mile radius. Addison was confident she would get it sold.

The phone began to ring. As Addison heard a female voice answer with a chipper tone, she knew there was no turning back.

"Hello, this is Martha O'Riley, your best-selling real estate agent, at your service. Who do I have the pleasure of speaking with?"

"Hi, Martha. My name is Addison Monroe. My mother, Mona Monroe, spoke highly of you."

Martha couldn't control herself; she butted in. "Oh, yes. Mona. What a lovely lady."

"Well, as you've probably heard, she recently passed. I am looking to put her store and house up for sale."

"Oh, heavens. Yes. I did hear of her passing, and I am sorry for your loss. Such dreadful news. I assure you, though, I will sell your properties. Can I stop by and see what we're working with? Will today or tomorrow do?"

"Sure. That would work. Can you meet me at the store in about twenty minutes?"

"I sure can. I am running to a meeting, but I will do a quick stop."

"I appreciate that. See you soon, Martha."

Martha hung up, and Addison mentally prepared herself for her arrival.

Addison lit a candle to make it smell nice, swept the floor, moved the boxes filled with her personal things out to her car, and went back in to wait for Martha.

It was half past the hour when a tall, thin, red head, dressed head to toe in her Sunday's best, came walking through the front door. Her hair was perfectly styled and hair sprayed, curled and layered to her shoulders; she was covered in jewelry; she had on two-inch pumps and entered with an infectious smile. Addison walked towards her.

"Hello. You must be Martha."

"Addison. How are you? I'm so sorry about your mother. I loved her. We all did. She was one of Edgerton's most adored residents. I was hoping there would be a funeral, so I could pay my respects." She leaned forward and gave Addison a hug.

Addison was startled by her hug, not knowing her. "Oh, thanks."

Martha quickly pulled away and then started looking around the store.

Addison bit her bottom lip and thought the comment over before responding. "Yeah, Mom didn't want a funeral or anything. She wanted to be remembered as a healthy person and in good spirits. She never did like funerals much. She made me promise that I wouldn't do anything, not even a memorial dinner. I can't break a promise."

"Well, I think a funeral is more for the living than the dead, but I understand. If those were her wishes, you have to abide by them. I respect that."

"I might take her ashes and scatter them in some of her favorite places. I haven't decided yet."

"That would be nice, dear. I must say, Addison, this place is a gem. A part of history. It is going to sell so fast."

"Great," Addison said.

"I would suggest one thing. We can do a one-time walkthrough, kind of like a Christmas open house. Do you have a few things you can decorate the store with? Nothing much, just for appeal. Maybe lights or a picture or two?"

"Actually, I have a small selection of things that I am getting appraised. Maybe I could have them for sale? They include some art pieces, illustrations, and a few rare antiques. Not a huge selection, but it might bring some of her old regulars in."

"That's a wonderful idea. Have a few snacks out. Mingle a little bit. We are bound to get an offer. This is prime real estate right here, honey."

"My mom always used to say that. She said that this place was a hot commodity, and she was the lucky person to have it."

"To tell you the truth, I am surprised you don't want to keep it."

"I thought about it, but I don't know how to run a store, and if I am honest, I'm not sure I want to."

"I understand that." Martha took out her phone and looked at the calendar. "Can you get the store ready in two days? I'll take pictures and get it posted online. I will post an ad about the event, and we will get this done before Christmas."

"That soon, huh? You really think you can get this sold by then?"

"I do."

"Okay. Wonderful. I trust you. Two days, it is."

Martha started whistling and then clapped her hands out of excitement. "I will get out of your hair and get working. Thank you, Addison. See you soon."

Addison put her hand up to wave goodbye. "Bye. Thanks, Martha."

Martha walked to the door, opened it, and walked out.

Addison's nerves went into over-drive, but she was up for the task. She took out a piece of paper and wrote down a checklist: get items appraised, mark their value, hang the paintings and illustrations against the wall, hang lights, and buy baked goods.

Addison pulled out a phone book from the drawer and called an appraiser.

A deep voice answered on the other end. "Hello."

"Hi. My name is Addison. I have a handful of antiques that need to be appraised, but I am on a tight deadline, and I need it done in the next forty-eight hours. Can you help me?"

"I can have my business partner come look at everything. Are you there now?"

"Yes, I am. I was just getting ready to leave, but if you are available, I will stay here."

"Edgerton isn't that busy with appraisals right now. I'll have Jed head over."

"Okay, thank you."

Addison hung up the phone. She was surprised by the quickness of everything. Everyone was steadfast in their work.

Pulling out the items she needed appraised, she set them out on the counter and floor. Within ten minutes, a young gentleman came through the door.

"Hello," he said.

"Hi, there. I'm assuming you are Jed?"

He shook his head yes.

"I'm Addison. Thank you for coming, especially on such short notice. I have everything over here by the counter. I'm not sure if any of it is worth anything, but I just want to make sure. There are a few paintings with the artist's initials on it and a few rare looking antiques ... maybe they are special?"

"Everything is special in its own right. Even if they are not worth something significant, I can give you an idea of what I would price it at."

"Yeah, that would be great. I'm going to try selling them."

"Perfect."

Jed looked over each item, looking closely at its rarity, aesthetic, desirability, authenticity, and condition.

"She has some really good pieces. These 8-point octagonal dummy doorknobs with cut glass, that are set on Yale Pasco cast iron plates, they are probably from about 1900 or 1905. Since you have pairs of 2, I'd sell them for $300 a pair."

"Great," said Addison. She wrote down the price on a little ticket and then moved them aside.

"These paintings ... I've never heard of this artist or seen this work before. And, these are great drawings, but I don't think they are worth anything much. They look like they were done in the last five to ten years. I would set whatever price you want for them. It might be a local artist."

"That's what I figured. They are so different than anything my mom normally collects. I was curious. One of them is on hold for a client. I told him he could have it. He was supposed to come in and grab it. It's amazing how many different styles of things my mom had in the shop."

"You know us collectors, we don't say no to anything. She must have liked the artist."

"Yeah, like you said, they are definitely special in their own right."

Jed picked up another antique. It was similar to the 19th century trade sign she gave Jack. "You could probably sell this anywhere from $700-1,500. I would start high."

"Whoa. I didn't realize something like that would be worth so much. I gave one away for free. See, this is why I didn't want to get rid of things on my own. I don't know anything about this stuff."

"Your mom must have traveled a lot and bought things online. Very rare, unique finds."

"She was consumed by these things. She lived for it. She followed in my grandmother's footsteps. Who knows, maybe some of this stuff has been here since my grandma ran the store."

"That's definitely a possibility. Like these mirrors." Jed pointed to a pair of gold mirror wall sconces. He checked the tag that her mom had placed on them as a description. "These are from Italy, circa 1740. Wow."

"How much for something like that?"

"The silvered glass, the wooden frame with silver leafing with acanthus metal candle arms and nozzles, the metal motifs in ribbons, palmettes, c-scrolls, floral and foliate, acanthus leaves, and rais-de-coeur … so rare and subtle. Pretty good condition, some minor losses and wear, including what seems to be a small old restoration and update on the color of the metal. I'd price this as a set at about $3,800-4,000."

Addison's eyes widened. She couldn't believe how much value these items had. They looked old, used, and worn. "I never would have imagined. Now I'm second guessing some of the things I sold to the other resale shops. I'm hoping they didn't lowball me. I did do my research, though, so I think Mom would be proud. Hopefully I didn't donate anything that was worth a lot."

Jed smirked. "Never throw away something in an antique shop until you get it looked at."

"Most of the donations were random household items … old baskets, rugs, cups, shelves … nothing that needed to be appraised. So, I feel pretty good about it."

He shook his head. "Oh, that makes sense. Yeah, that kind of stuff can be donated."

"I have learned my lesson, though, never again will I call this stuff junk. Some of it is worth a pretty penny." Addison laughed.

"This scraper here is pretty cool."

Addison slightly jumped. "Scraper?"

"Yes, it's a handheld. About 15" in length, 4" wide. Nice wooden handle."

"Can I see that, please?"

Jed handed it to her. "I can't believe I had it in this pile all this time. Not what I would have imagined a scraper to look like. I'm going to hang on to this one."

"Sure," Jed said. He continued, going item by item, writing prices down after scanning its appearance and origin. In total, the group of stuff valued at about ten thousand dollars. She kept the paintings separate and priced them with the illustrations as a package deal. Two thousand dollars for all of it, supplies included.

As Jed finished up, he wished Addison well and said goodbye.

After the door closed, Addison went and locked it. She turned off the light, turned her back to the door and rested upon it, looking at the shop in its entirety. She was overcome. The whole day was exhausting yet fulfilling, having accomplished so much. Tears began falling down her cheek. "It's done, Mom," she whispered into the empty space. Wiping her eyes, she headed to the back door, locked up, and went to her car.

When she arrived home, she went upstairs. Taking out the slip of paper with Jack's number written on it, she sat on the edge of the bed and called it. She was a bit nervous thinking about hearing his voice again. Ring after ring, she grew more anxious. But there was no answer, just a generic answering machine beep to leave a message. Addison took a deep breath and thought of what to say. She remembered that Jack asked her not to mention the antiques on the phone, so his dad didn't catch on. She had to be discreet. As the beep ended and there was silence for her to speak, she sat up straight. "Hi, this is Addison. I am calling for Jack. Jack, I have something of yours. If you could, please stop and see me in town. Thanks."

Addison was disappointed that she didn't hear his voice. She was excited about the thought of re-connecting with him. She hoped he would listen to the message and come see her. She could use another friendly distraction.

Chapter 5: Closing Up Shop

The words "Open House" were written in large letters on a sign outside of the shop. Three balloons were tied to the sign, blowing in the cold, brisk wind. Addison showed up early to set up. She filled the counter with Bob Costello's sugary sweets, brewed a fresh pot of coffee, set out waters, and laid out the sales items. Dangling a string of white lights around the counter and another in the window-scape, it felt welcoming. She propped the door open, letting the cool air blow in. It felt good having a draft.

Addison could hear Martha's voice in the distance, echoing from the street as she walked up to the entrance, bringing along a few work associates. Martha was pleasantly surprised by the lights and the set-up. Pushing the door open, she walked in with big energy and big hair. "Addison, hello. The place looks great. Expect a great turnout. I marketed the heck out of this place."

Addison smiled politely and stood to the side. "Hello, everyone."

Many townsfolk came through the doors, one after the other. They did a walk-through, scanned the items, nibbled on food, and left. A few regulars stopped in, buying an antique or two. As Addison chatted up one of her mom's old acquaintances, the phone rang. She excused herself, went behind the counter, and picked up the phone.

"Hello."

"Hi, is this Mona's Antiques?"

"Yes, this is."

"To my knowledge, you have a collection from a local artist. The initials are JB. Is that correct?"

"Oh, yes. Do you know the name?"

"I'm actually calling on behalf of my client. They would like me to put a bid in for the collection."

"It's not really a bid. You can buy everything, supplies included, for two thousand."

"Steep price, but we will take it."

Addison swallowed, feeling like she had a lump in her throat. She was surprised that someone wanted it, let alone, for that much. "Okay. I will put it near the front of the store. If you can swing out tonight, you can have it."

"That would be great. I will be there within the hour."

"Perfect. I will have it ready for you. Bye."

As Addison hung up, she noticed a man talking to Martha. His back was facing her, but if she had to bet, it was Jack. She could tell by the hair, the height, the build, and the voice. Addison immediately filled with nerves, feeling jittery. She straightened her shirt and pulled her hair to the side. Licking her lips, she walked slowly over to him.

Tapping him on the shoulder, he turned around and met her face to face.

"Addison, hi."

"Jack, I thought that was you."

"I got your message."

"I found your scraper."

"No way. You did?"

"Yeah. And I wanted to make sure you got your painting. I put them aside for you."

"I can't believe how much work you have done in here. It's empty."

"It was a lot. Quite cathartic."

"I bet."

"I was hoping you would bring your dad. I thought maybe he would enjoy some of these items I am selling. I had an appraiser come and price everything out. By the way, I gave you quite a good antique. It's worth a decent amount. You better hold on to it."

"Do you want it back? It's fine. I can grab it."

"No. Of course not. Did your dad enjoy it?"

"Yes, he did. It made him smile. I wish I could bottle that up and give it to him every day. He has been so depressed."

"Maybe it's the weather?"

"I can't place it exactly."

"I'll pray that he feels like himself again."

"I appreciate that."

Addison put her hand on his arm. "Feel free to help yourself to food and drink."

"I'm good but thank you."

Addison smiled. "If you will excuse me, Aunt Wanda just came in. I'm going to say hello real fast."

"Oh, by all means, do as you must."

Addison walked up to Wanda with a big smile. She put her arms out to signal a hug.

"Addy cakes, this is sad. I can't believe it. I didn't think it would look like this so soon. I would have helped."

"I know. Once I started, I couldn't stop."

"Martha is the best realtor in town. I wouldn't be surprised if it was sold by tomorrow."

"Let's hope. Aunt Wanda, if you want something, you don't have to pay for it, feel free to take what you want."

"Oh, darling, thank you."

Wanda walked over to the sales items and scanned everything. "I can't believe this is all that's left. If you don't mind, I'm going to take this tea strainer."

"It's all yours." Addison picked it up and handed it to Wanda.

"I have to go, but I appreciate it. I'm glad I got to see the shop one last time. Have you thought about Christmas Eve yet, sweetheart?" Wanda asked.

"I will take up you on it. I would love to come over," Addison said.

"That is the best news I have heard in a long time. We will set a place for you."

Addison leaned forward, hugged her, and gave her a slight kiss on the cheek. "See you then."

As Wanda walked out, many of the prospective buyers left as well. Martha was getting ready to end the open house. "Addison, I have a few interested parties. I will call you and let you know if I get an offer. I might be able to print it off tonight, if I get what I think."

"Thank you, Martha."

"It was a big success. Have a great night."

Martha walked out, waving as she exited.

A tall, slender woman popped her head in the door, looking for something.

Addison walked over to her. "Can I help you?"

"I called on the phone. I am picking up the art."

"Oh, yes. They are right there in the corner. I put them aside for you."

The lady passed Addison an envelope. "This is the money. Thank you for doing business. Have a great night."

Addison was delighted and relieved that the art was sold. "You, too."

As the lady left, Addison shut the door and looked around. Jack was the only one left. She walked towards him. "I should have asked her a little bit more about the paintings. Something about it intrigues me. It seems so mysterious."

Jack was silent.

Feeling the need to make him comfortable, Addison kept talking. "Well, it's down to you and me."

"I should probably get out of your way too. I just didn't want to leave without saying a real goodbye."

"You want some coffee? A danish or a cookie? I don't want all of this to go to waste."

Jack tilted his head, bit his bottom lip, and thought for a moment. "Sure, why not."

"I don't have chairs in here anymore, so we can hop up on the counter and sit."

"Rebels," Jack said.

Addison propped herself up. "That's better. My feet are killing me. Well, Jack, what's new?"

Jack propped himself up, as well. "Not much. I headed back to Waterford to check on things, but I came right back, because I didn't feel right leaving my dad in the condition he is in. I wish I could get him in better spirits."

"You are a good guy."

"Eh ... the animals needed tending to, anyway."

Addison smiled and then looked out the window. She knew he was just being modest. "Wow, it's really starting to come down now. At first, they said only an inch or two, but it's looking like a lot more. It always feels like Christmastime when it snows. It's one of the only times I truly enjoy it."

"They projected it to go south, but you know how that goes; they are not always right."

"I need to dig out a shovel."

"I wouldn't worry about it. The plows and village workers will be through here by morning. I'm sure it will stop soon."

Addison took her sights back to Jack, handsome and endearing. "Jack, tell me about yourself. How was your childhood? I bet you were the cutest."

"I'm guessing it wasn't much different than yours. Simple, small town life. I was relatively popular. I was friends with just about everyone. I didn't really have a set group of friends, besides a few neighbors that did farming club with me."

Addison stared at him, watching his mannerisms and mouth move. She was intrigued. She interrupted. "Then, you had a much better childhood than me. I'm not sure why I had such a rough time with friends growing up. I never really clicked with a set group of people. Maybe that's why I wanted to leave. Don't get me wrong, I had friends, but it wasn't that happy, free-spirited childhood that most people dream of; going to dances, playing sports, having non-stop play dates, it didn't happen for me. And by the time I was independent and free to make my own choices, my father passed. I became reclusive. I had to grow up fast, and I didn't see myself in any of the other kids my age. When they would talk about things, I didn't connect or relate."

"That makes sense. You went through an experience that they didn't. It shaped you; it changed you."

"Yeah, exactly."

Jack was just as intrigued. "Not to change the subject, but I am interested. Since you moved away, and you love the city so much, what is your favorite part of New York?"

Addison smiled, about to say something. Then, she stopped. "Well, have you ever been there?"

"Once. When I was a kid. It was like nothing I had ever seen before. It is huge. But I am not a city guy. I don't like crowds."

"That doesn't surprise me."

"Why do you say that?"

"The way you carry yourself, your clothes, your attitude, your calmness. I just see you as a country guy, not wanting to be around many people. You have this laid-back nature about you."

"A country guy and a city girl, sitting on a counter talking about life. Isn't that something."

"And it doesn't feel wrong," Addison said, blushing.

She couldn't believe she just said that out loud.

Jack took a sip of his coffee and shook his head, agreeing with her. "I can't disagree with you."

"Isn't life weird? Things you plan for, they never pan out exactly the way you want them to. But when you stop thinking, when you stop looking, when you just live, minute by minute, things happen naturally, as they should, and it feels like the most right thing in the world."

"I do have to point out, though, you weren't always a city girl. There's a bit of country girl in you. And some would say that since you grew up here and spent more time here than there, you are more country girl than city girl."

Addison laughed. "Touché."

"You might not like the sound of that, but I have to point out the obvious. Never ignore your roots."

"I have to say, being back here, it's nice. It's better than I remembered. It's pretty special. I never thought those words would come out of my mouth."

"Nice to hear you say that."

"Now, getting back to your question about New York. For starters, I love everything. I love Midtown where tourists gather in crowds and fill the streets. There's so much excitement and energy there. The Theater District is lively. It's historical. And I love Central Park. I could walk that for days and sit and people watch. It's so beautiful. SoHo with its boutiques and high-end art. It draws me in, especially at night. There are great hotspots. It's also one of my favorite places to check out for the street vendors. I bought one of my favorite bracelets there right after I moved. Don't get me started on Little Italy. It's a dream. The pizza, the pasta, the bakeries ... there's nothing like it. My mouth might start watering just talking about it. Mulberry Street and Old St. Patrick's Cathedral ... they are musts. The residents have so much pride, it feels like you are actually in Italy. Greenwich Village holds a soft place in my heart, too, because I spent a lot of time there during college. A friend of mine lived near Washington Square. She has since moved back home, so I don't see her anymore, but some of my best memories were with her. Upper East Side is so posh and wealthy. It's what I strive for. The brownstones and high-rises, the museums ... maybe one day."

"Is that what you want? To be posh and wealthy?"

"When you say it like that, it sounds bad."

"It's just a question, not a judgment."

91

Addison stopped herself from talking further. She took offense to his question. She wasn't uppity and didn't wish for unreasonable things. She just wanted to feel success and independence; a fulfillment of some-kind. If allowed, she could talk about the city all night. It was special to her. It fueled her. There were so many great things she had discovered about it, being there the last five years. And it didn't come easy; she'd had many difficult bumps in the road along the way. But she feared he wouldn't understand. She shifted the conversation in a different direction.

"Let's talk about you," she said.

"I'm a simple guy. What you see is what you get. I'm honest; I'm loyal, and I'm straight-forward. Some people don't like that because I say it how it is. But I want the best for everyone around me. I want to connect to people. I want to help others. I want to make a difference. Overall, I just want to spend time in nature. I want to keep things in my life organic and feel grounded."

Addison listened to him closely. She couldn't believe how self-aware he was. She could barely figure out what outfit to wear each morning, let alone decipher who she was at the core. She felt like she was still constantly discovering things about herself. What did that say about her? What was she missing? Were her priorities completely off? He had himself all figured out. "Do you look towards the future then, or do you just take it day by day?" she asked.

"A little of both. I look to the future only to manifest my hopes, goals, and dreams. Most days, I don't worry about things. I don't put pressure on myself. I don't get upset when things don't happen the way I want them to. I just move through it and have faith that everything will work out in its own time. The reality is, I am a busy body. I will always be doing something, taking care of something, fixing something. I work hard. I'm relatively easy to please. I'm a patient man. It doesn't take a lot to make me happy. But I look for realness. I'm at the point in my life where I don't want to pretend. I don't want to put on a front. I want genuine conversation, relationships, and moments."

"What do you enjoy doing?" Addison asked. She was so taken with him and his directness. He was a good person. His kindness, his outlook, his soulfulness, she could see it in his eyes, and it radiated through his voice and words. He was honest, and he was a gentleman.

"I enjoy quiet nights looking at the stars. I enjoy busy days tending to my animals. I enjoy a nice warm meal, a good fire, the heat of the sun, a nice walk, a gentle breeze, a ride around the property."

"You make me want the same when you explain it that way."

"Haven't you ever just slowed down and allowed life to happen? Enjoying the things that most people take for granted?"

"Not really. I need to know what's going to happen next. I'm not good with the unknown. Maybe it's due to the trauma of my past."

"Does that cause issues when dating?"

"Yeah, for sure. I get way ahead of myself. I have to admit, I pick the wrong people. I jump into things too fast. It's always so surface level. I think I have had a hard time allowing anyone to get to know the real me. I haven't always felt worthy of love, yet I have wanted it so badly. If I'm truthful, I settle. I think I can change people. I try to conform to being someone that they want me to be, and in the end, I find myself extremely unhappy and unseen. I have learned to set my standards and love myself more. But now I'm in this place where I'm nervous. I don't want anyone telling me what to do. I want to have my own voice. I want my own career. In a sense, that's a form of control for me to keep things in line."

"I'd say you've learned a lot through dating, and you seem ready now. Maybe, just let it happen naturally, and allow the right person in."

"How will I know when it's the right person? That's the question."

Jack raised his eyebrows and smiled. "Hmm … Well, I'm not sure there's an exact answer to that. I just believe you will know. It will feel right, and you will have the same values, morals, and desires towards the future. I think there has to be a good foundation of friendship, a depth in the connection and conversation, a balance to each personality, a likability factor that also creates attraction, and at the end of the day, you respect and love one another; so much so, that you can't get enough of that person. That person, essentially, becomes your person, and you don't want to be without them."

"So, you never worry about such things? I'm crazy, huh?"

"I can tell you are afraid. Don't be. You are wise enough to know better at this point in your life. You know the qualities you are looking for. Don't accept anything less. The fear of what could be is limiting you from getting it."

"Are you sure you are not a therapist?" Addison laughed.

"I deal with people on a daily basis. I see the way people communicate with one another. I'd like to share my life with someone, but I want it to come on its own. I don't want to control it. I want it to be natural, like I suggested to you. I don't want to force anything. I would rather be alone than be with someone that doesn't know for sure if they want to be there. I don't want to nitpick each other every day or talk ill of one another when the other person isn't around. I'm ready to give my heart to someone, but they have to be ready to reciprocate equally with an open heart and an open mind. I understand everyone has a past, but I don't want to constantly relive it or feel held back by it. There has to be an innate sense of trust and loyalty. Relationships aren't easy, I know that. I need someone that is understanding of my long work hours and that's willing to adjust and adapt. They need to have their own independence, beyond me. I will treat my partner like a queen, but I, specifically, can't create their happiness. I can play a part and add to it, but that's all. I don't want to be solely responsible for it. That's too much."

Addison shook her head, agreeing with him. "Yeah." She didn't have words. She allowed what he said to sink in and marinate. Everything he said made so much sense.

Knowing he struck a chord with her and seeing that she grew silent, Jack felt it necessary to lighten the mood again. "Is New York where you see yourself living forever?"

"I wouldn't say that. I am open. If an opportunity takes me somewhere else, I'd consider it. Hopefully, it would be near a beach, but I'm not picky."

"So, you are a beach person?"

"I love water. Anywhere near water."

"I like water too. There's something quite relaxing about it. Listening to the creek near my house, it's soothing. One of my favorite things to do on a rainy day is lay in my room with the windows cracked open. I listen to the storm blow through. And I have a pond that I can canoe or kayak on. It's relaxing. It might not be the ocean, but it is still beautiful."

"That sounds perfect. We live close enough to the ocean; it is only a short drive."

"Exactly. See, that's the kind of positive attitude I love."

Addison smiled listening to him talk and hearing him say the word love, even if it wasn't directed at her. She imagined it in her head. He exuded realness and provided such a sense of clarity to the conversation. The more they got to know each other, the more they enjoyed themselves. Hours passed as they talked through their wishes and wants. They discussed the world, good and bad. They laughed through lighthearted jokes and sarcasm. They didn't notice the time. It practically stood still.

Mid conversation, Jack's phone began ringing. He looked down. "It's my dad."

Addison smiled. "Answer it, please. He's probably worried about you."

"I'm a grown adult."

Addison laughed. "We might do the same to our kids one day."

Jack shook his head in agreement and then answered. "Hello." Jack shook his head, listening to his dad speak. "I'll check, Dad. It wasn't supposed to get that bad. I got caught up in town. I'll be careful. Go to bed and get some sleep."

As Jack hung up, he looked at Addison. "The news reported some heavy snowfall. Since I didn't come home yet, he was worried about me. I guess they warned people not to drive on the country roads unless absolutely necessary, so the plows can do their job."

Addison scooted herself off the counter and headed towards the window. Looking out, she dropped her jaw, opening her mouth in awe. "It's a winter wonderland."

Jack followed. Standing next to her, he side-eyed her, giving her a sly smile. "The news was right; the weatherman was wrong. This is starting to look like a blizzard."

"I'm sorry, we were talking so long, and we got caught up. I didn't realize it would be a difficult drive home for you."

"I quite enjoyed it. I always enjoy my time with you."

Addison loved hearing him say that. It took her breath away and made her throat dry, feeling caught up in the moment. Swallowing and fidgeting with her hands, she looked at him. "Me, too. It has been quite the surprise."

Addison went to the door and opened it. A pile of snow that was resting up against it fell forward onto the wood floor. "Wow, it's really windy. It has picked up. There's lots of snow, but it's still coming down pretty heavy." She took her foot and swiped the snow from the wood floor back outside.

Jack had his dad's worries playing out in his head. "Maybe I should stay in town at the B&B? I can give them a call and see if they have a room. It's late. I didn't realize it was so late. I'd call my buddy Timothy, he has a big truck and plow, but he's been working about an hour South of here. And with these storms, I'm sure he will be busy. They probably haven't salted or anything yet."

"Well …" Addison bit her bottom lip contemplating something.

"Yes? It looks like you have something on your mind."

"You can stay with me." Addison put her hands up and raised her shoulders, scrunching her face. "We have an attached guest house. You can get to it from the breezeway. The house is in walking distance from here, so we don't need a car. Plenty of room, and we won't get in each other's way. If you stay in the guest house, you can have all the privacy you desire. Way better than a hotel. You won't have to stay with strangers. It has its own bathroom. The only thing you have to come in the house for is the kitchen."

"Quite an imposition."

"No. It's really not. And, if my mom was still here, she would insist upon it. We are friends now, aren't we?"

Jack smiled. "Yeah, okay. I'll get out of your hair first thing in the morning."

"Great. I mean, not that you have to leave in a rush, first thing in the morning, just great that you don't feel awkward staying. It makes me feel better that you won't be driving and that you are not spending money on a hotel room."

Jack knew she was flustered. Her words were running together. "Want to get going then, before we get stuck here?"

"Yeah, that's a good idea. I can only imagine that these wood floors feel as hard as they look. I'm not sure my back could take it. And sleeping in here would be awfully cold without blankets."

"You? What about me? I'm older than you."

"By how much, do you think? Cause we've never brought it up. I would say you are thirty-five, give or take?" Addison squinted her eyes thinking it over.

Jack smiled. "Close. I'd say you are twenty-five-ish."

"What's ish mean?" Addison playfully asked, gently and playfully smacking him in the arm.

Addison locked up, turned the lights off, and went out the back door. Jack followed her. They fastened their jackets, put gloves and hats on, and tied their scarves. "I usually go out the front door if I'm walking, but I left my car back here. I put a bunch of stuff in it today. I'll leave it here, but I want to lock it."

Addison walked up to her car and pressed the lock button, activating its alarm. "Okay, where were we? You were calling me an old lady, and I was about to throw a snowball at you." Addison leaned down and grabbed a handful of snow. "Watch what you say now. I am armed."

Jack flinched, acting playful. "I don't know exactly how old you are. I figure you are somewhere near your mid-twenties. I don't want to guess and get myself in more trouble."

"If you had to guess, what would you say?" Addison raised her hand, showing the snowball resting upon her mitten.

"Twenty-four."

"Close. But you are wrong. And you are too high, so I'm sorry, but I have to do this." Addison threw the snowball at him.

Putting his hands up, in awe and shock, Jack's mouth dropped, and he swiped the snow away from his hair, face, and jacket. "You don't know what you started. You better run."

Addison's eyes widened from anticipation and fear. "Oh, no," she said. She turned away from him and started running, letting out a playful shriek.

Jack leaned down in a fast manner, grabbed two handfuls of cold, wet snow and charged at her, throwing it at her back.

"AHH, that's freezing. It went down my shirt."

Jack started laughing. "Okay, we are even."

"It depends. We each have one more guess. If you lose, you have to do a snow angel."

"A snow angel? I haven't done one of those since I was, like, 7."

"Live a little," Addison taunted.

"You go first," he said.

She looked at him, taking in the features of his face, trying to find wrinkles or age lines. He was quite adorable. "It's hard to tell. You look good for your age, whatever that might be. But you said I was close, so I'm going to guess that you are 33."

Jack shook his head side to side and gave her a side smirk. "Someone is doing a snow angel."

Addison shrieked. "I asked for it, so I guess I deserve it. But, before I do, I want to see if you are doing one with me. What is your final guess?"

Jack looked at her and answered surely. "Twenty-three."

Addison was annoyed. "Eh ... how? ... that is not fair."

"I listen. You said you went to NYU, and you stayed after you graduated, but that you have only been there for five years. So, I'd say that is right around twenty-two, twenty-three, twenty-four. And, besides, you already said no to twenty-five and twenty-four. I'm just going down from there."

Addison laughed, but she was impressed. "Wow. I either need to ask you more questions or be a better listener."

Jack laughed. "I'm awaiting your snow angel."

In the middle of a large open space, almost to her house, Addison laid down in the snow and moved her arms and legs back and forth, making an angel-like figure with her body. She started laughing, feeling like a little kid. "I need help getting up. I'm laughing too hard."

Jack went next to her and gave her his hand. "The most beautiful twenty-three-year old angel I have ever seen."

Addison was taken with his kindness, soft remarks, and admiration for her. She blushed once again and wiped off the snow from her clothing. He made her feel so good about herself. "Phew ... it's cold."

Putting his hands on the sides of her arms, he rubbed them in a fast motion, trying to create friction and heat. "I'm thirty-one, by the way," said Jack. He was concerned it might scare her off. It was a large age gap.

"It's becoming. Your maturity is one of the things I like the most about you. Tell me, Jack, why on Earth are you single?"

"I have high standards. I guess I'd say I'm kind of picky. I was engaged once. When that fell through, I told myself that I wouldn't search for it. It has to feel right. It has to be right. I'm looking for more than a physical attraction. I haven't found it yet so far, but I'm hopeful. I want a family. I want a wife and kids. I want to build a life with someone. I want that commitment. Everyone that knows me can basically confirm that. I'm true to the ones I care about, and I will devote myself to the person I choose. She has to be special. Someone that knocks me off my feet and gets me to think. It matters to me how my partner treats others."

Addison wasn't sure if he was hinting at something, directing it at her, or if that's just what she was hoping for. She didn't want to be presumptuous and get her hopes up or say anything to embarrass herself. She immediately changed the conversation. Something she was getting really good at. "Right around this path, which you can't see right now because it's covered in snow, is the house. We just have to veer around to the front."

Jack knew Addison was ignoring his remarks. He knew that she had a hard time taking to his romantic advances, believing them to be true. He was sure of himself and his words, but he didn't want to take it too far or make her feel overwhelmed. Her hesitance and non-response made him feel uneasy. He felt alone in his feelings. He needed to remain patient and assure her of his character.

Taking a step forward, Addison's boot filled with snow. It got stuck, and she couldn't pull it out. Her foot came up, but the boot stayed in place. "Uh-oh," she said.

"What is it?" Jack asked.

"My boot. I lost my boot. And it's freezing."

"Get on. I'll give you a piggy back ride and carry you up to the door."

"Are you sure?"

"Get on."

Addison went behind him and grabbed ahold of his shoulders, pulling up on him, hopping onto his back, and straddling him, wrapping her legs around his waist. "I'm too old for this." She giggled, feeling foolish.

"No one is ever too old. It's the person carrying the person that you have to worry about. If I'm fine, there's no need to worry. And we just established, you are a young chicken. I'm an old cow."

"I like your animal analogies, Dr., but nonetheless, it's kind of embarrassing."

"You might be embarrassed, but why? I'm in this with you. And, no one is around. It's not embarrassing to me, so you shouldn't worry about such things."

Addison was realizing that she didn't need to have her guard up. He was non-judgmental. He didn't care about such things. Image wasn't important. She could be herself, completely and utterly herself. It wasn't something she was used to. It felt nice to let go and be carefree, without worry.

Being so close to his hair, as it flipped up in the back ever so slightly near her face, tickling her cheek, she could feel the endorphins. His natural smell got her every time. His neck, which was the perfect spot to snuggle her nose into ... his ears, perfectly shaped and pleasing to the eye ... his broad shoulders, strong, brawny, and defined ... it put her into a tizzy, thinking risqué thoughts. She felt the strength of his stomach muscles and arms as she held tightly around his body. He exuded the perfect balance of masculine energy and warmth. Being that close to him made her feel electrified with energy. The depth of his voice and the vibration it let off when he spoke went through her. The softness of his demeanor, the safety of his hands as they held her legs close to him ... it was all too much, overwhelming her senses and heightening her imagination. She licked and bit her bottom lip as her thoughts went wild.

Walking up the steps, getting to the door, Jack gently let her down. As she slowly came to, realizing she was in fantasy land, she tried turning it off, so he wouldn't catch on. Her hands touched his, ever so slightly, as she tried gaining her balance. Their hands fit each other's perfectly. His, sturdy and strong, hers, dainty and gentle.

Addison looked at him, hopping around on one foot. She was sure there was a twinkle in her eye and was a bit embarrassed by her thoughts. *If he only knew.* "Thank you. I need to get these socks off. My toes are freezing."

Grabbing her keys out of her pocket, she unlocked the door. As she walked in and turned the light on, she felt happy. Having someone with her made her feel comfortable. Taking her socks off and throwing them to the side, she moved over, allowing Jack to come in to take his shoes off. "Well, this is it." She moved behind him and reached around to close the door. "I will show you around, and then I will get the guest house ready for you."

Jack smiled. "Great."

"Why don't you follow me," Addison suggested.

Addison didn't want to admit it, but she was tempted by his presence. She was taken by his aura. It was taking all of her self-restraint to hold back. Being alone with him made it worse. Knowing there was no one to interrupt them, knowing there were no boundaries and no separation, it left her feeling uneasy in her skin. What stopped her was the fact that he hadn't shown any interest, thus far, in moving forward, besides simple little flirty comments. She didn't want him to feel uncomfortable in her house, and she didn't want to make the first move. What if she was overthinking it?

What if he really didn't think of her like that? Distracting herself and easing the tension she had built up inside of her, she went into hostess mode.

Jack walked behind her, taking in each room. As they got to the kitchen and laundry room area, Addison opened a cabinet and pulled out a small kit of goodies: towels, toiletries, and an extra blanket and pillow. There was a walkthrough that connected to a large living area. They headed in there, and Addison turned around with delight.

"This is your room for the night. The mini fridge is stocked with waters. I just had the cleaning lady here. Everything is freshly washed and cleaned. The bathroom is immaculate. I brought you some extra soap, toilet paper, and towels. There's a hamper for dirty stuff, if you want me to wash something. The bed is good to go, but I thought you might like an extra pillow and blanket. Just in case. It is a bit chilly outside. I will turn the heat up. You have your own setting, so you can adjust it to your liking."

Jack was amused with her hosting abilities and charm. "Addison, I'm good. Thank you."

She smiled, knowing she was being a bit much. "You are welcome."

She went to leave and then stopped herself. Heading back into the room, she addressed him. "Jack, make yourself comfortable. Please don't be shy. You can use the kitchen any time you want."

"Seeing that you gave me all those baked goods, I'll be fine for a while."

"Okay then, good night."

"Night." Jack turned towards the bed and walked to the night table, setting his wallet down.

Addison was halfway down the breezeway when she stopped again. Something kept pulling her back to him. Walking back and peeking her head in, she whispered so she didn't scare him. "Jack?"

He turned. "You are back already?"

"Are you tired?"

Jack raised his left cheek and lip. "A little, but not too bad."

"Oh, okay. I was just going to say ... if you wanted to and you are not ready to go to sleep, since there's no tv in here, you can come in the family room and watch something."

Jack knew she wanted to spend more time with him, and he felt the same way. He felt flattered. "Yeah, I'd like that. I'm going to give my dad a call real fast and let him know I won't be home."

"Great, I could use the company. The quietness of the house is torture," Addison admitted.

"I was hoping it was because you couldn't get enough of me," Jack said with a playful smile.

Addison laughed. "That too." *He couldn't be more right.*

Addison waited by the doorway while Jack called his dad. She watched his lips move as he spoke, making her squirm. She needed to get out of the bedroom, so she wasn't tempted. As Jack hung up, he looked at her and raised his eyebrows. "Okay, where were we?"

Addison snapped herself out of her trance. "Huh? What?"

"We were planning on watching tv together, right?"

"Oh. Yeah. Sorry. Let's go." Addison turned around and started walking towards the breezeway. She took a deep breath and calmed herself.

As they entered the kitchen, Addison looked around, thinking of snacks. "Are you sure you don't want anything? Popcorn, frozen pizza, pancakes, eggs? You name it, I will make it."

"Quite the selection ... err ... yeah, I'll have eggs. That actually sounds good."

"Eggs, it is. They are probably not as fresh as the ones you are used to. They are from the store."

"That's okay. But I'll bring you some the next time I come out."

"How do you like yours cooked?"

"Scrambled."

"Really? I had you pegged as a sunny side up kind of guy."

"I like them simple. A little bit of salt and pepper, sometimes with cheese."

"Easy enough. I have to say, your laid back, easy going personality is something I find refreshing. You are going to make a wife very happy someday. You make it easy for someone to be around you. It would be easy to take care of you."

"Oh yeah?" he looked at her intently.

"I just mean …"

"I know what you mean. I have been told that more than once."

"If you allowed for it, I bet you would have many prospective suitors."

"Nah."

"Have you been in a lot of relationships?"

"One serious, long relationship. We were high school sweethearts. I loved being in a relationship. I like being with one person."

"What happened?"

"We grew apart. We wanted different things. We are still friends. It's better that way; we realized we weren't meant for one another."

"The one you were engaged to, I presume?"

"Yep, that's the one. At the time, I didn't have enough life experience to know myself or what I wanted. I wasn't fully aware of her needs and desire to grow. She was also a country girl that couldn't wait to get out of here. She needed to find herself. And I needed to focus on myself, learning my faults and realizing my part in all of it. I was maybe a bit selfish; I took her for granted. I have learned a lot since then."

"I believe most people need to become a whole person before giving themselves away in full. I respect that answer."

"Yeah, we met really young, and we both changed along the way. It was a difficult break-up, but it was necessary. How about you? What's your relationship history?"

"I have had three serious boyfriends, a few casual short ones, but nothing substantial enough to get me to commit."

"Are you afraid of commitment?"

Addison was beating the eggs, ignoring eye contact. She poured the bowl's contents into the buttered pan.

Jack came up behind her. He took the pepper and salt and dashed it into the pan. Being so close to one another, the energy was heightened. Jack, being a gentleman, stepped back and gave her space. "What are you looking for?" he asked.

"I want someone that makes me want to stay in one place. I've never had that before. But also, someone that doesn't hold me back, that accepts all of me. I would love to have a significant other that wants to experience new things with me. A person that makes me feel alive and fills me with hope. I want a partner that equally wants the same thing. I want them to adore me in such a way that I feel it every time they look at me. Someone dependable, secure, honest, loyal, adventurous, and above all, someone that makes me laugh ... I think that's so important."

Jack interjected. "So, me, basically ..."

Addison lost her breath and coughed. She turned and looked at him. "Presumptuous and confident."

"I'm kidding, I'm kidding." He started laughing.

They both knew he wasn't kidding, and they both knew they liked each other. They just couldn't say it out loud. The attraction to one another was certain and clear.

Addison was feeling spellbound by his presence and protective of her heart. "Jack, why don't you go put something on the tv for us to watch. Relax. I'll bring the food in."

Jack knew she was deflecting. "Addison ..."

"Go ahead. I like anything. You pick."

He went up behind her, his chest to her back. The hair on her arms stood up. She had tingles all down her body. She closed her eyes and swallowed. He made her feel a way that she had never felt. It scared her. It was deep. Heart-pulling deep. What would happen to her life if she allowed it to go further? She was just starting to get somewhere at work, and she didn't want to carry on a long-distance relationship. Personality and connection wise, it felt right. Logistically and life plan wise, it felt like a mess.

"I didn't mean to make you feel uncomfortable. I was just joking. I didn't mean to startle you or weird you out," Jack said. His voice was soft, soothing, kind, and loving.

Addison tried to brush it off using the opposite approach. She stayed still, not wanting to make any moves to hint at anything. In a fast, loud, high voice, she spoke back. "No, you didn't. It's okay. I knew you were playing around."

He put his hands on the sides of her arms and squeezed them gently before walking into the family room. Addison was filled with nervous energy. She wasn't sure why it was so hard for her to let go and allow it to happen, when she knew that she wanted it so badly. Why was she suppressing her feelings? She wanted so badly to turn around and kiss him, passionately and without concern of time. For him to hold her in his arms and never let go. To feel as one, to be wrapped up in his eyes and feel his mouth upon hers, and feel each other's skin touching, body to body. She just didn't know if it was the right thing to do. If she did, would it be a one-night thing? Would they ruin the connection they were building, going too fast? Ignoring her desires, she finished the eggs, separated them onto two plates, and went in the family room to see him. Maybe she was thinking too much? Maybe she just needed to be in the moment …

If she was honest, he took her breath away. More than anyone ever had. His energy was all-consuming, leaving her foggy brained, unable to concentrate on much else. The glances between them grew to be flirtatious in nature with a humorous undertone. Everything was lighthearted. But it didn't go beyond that. He might be the most respectful man she had ever been around. He treated her with such dignity and honor. Yet, the more connected she felt to him, her insecurities and fears crept in. The fear of being hurt didn't sit well with her. Losing another loved one would break her. Especially a man.

Addison always wanted to find someone that took her in with his eyes and made her feel alive and desired. The way Jack looked at her was unnerving. He took her in, deeply, connecting soul to soul. He really listened to her and paid attention to her. He wanted to get to know her. When he saw her across the room, she could feel his admiration and gaze. But he was never inappropriate or selfish about it. He was mannerly and gracious. No one had ever gotten to her this fast before. She wasn't sure how to process it. Was it real or was all of the relationship talk going to her head?

Addison tried snapping herself out of her mental imagery. "Eggs are done. Hope you are still hungry," she said cheerfully, awaiting Jack's response and help. As Addison walked around the back of the couch to the front table, she noticed Jack sleeping. His eyes were closed, and he was breathing more heavily. While she was a tad disappointed, overall, it gave her a sense of happiness and relief. There was no pressure, no awkwardness, no worries or anticipation of where the night would take them. He was comfortably sleeping under the same roof as her, and it felt good having a man in the house. She felt safe. He looked so peaceful. She adored him as she looked over his face. Not wanting to wake him, making him move to the guest house, she set down the plates. Picking up a blanket from the basket next to the fireplace, she went up close to him and covered him, keeping him warm. She picked up the remote and turned the volume down and then went to the wall to dim the lights.

Addison was tired. She didn't want to eat anymore. She picked up the plates, went into the kitchen, and set them in the refrigerator. Then, she rubbed her eyes and made her way upstairs to her bed. After changing and brushing her teeth, she pulled the comforter back and laid down, ready to go to sleep. She left the door open just in case Jack woke up and needed something. Tiredness hit her hard, and she fell asleep quickly as her head rested on the pillow.

Chapter 6: Feels Like Home

It was the crack of dawn. Addison woke up, startled from a loud sound outside. Taking her eye mask off, stretching, and getting out of bed, she pulled the curtain back and looked down, noticing Jack. He was all bundled up, working hard on clearing the driveway. Cracking the window open, she yelled down.

"Good morning."

Jack stopped what he was doing and looked up with a smile. "Good morning."

Addison loved the sound of his deep, sensual voice. "Aren't you cold?"

"It could be worse. All of this shoveling is keeping me warm."

"How did you get a shovel? And, you don't have to do that, you know."

"I found it in the garage. I hope you don't mind. And, yes, I did have to. I wasn't about to let you."

"I'm actually a good shoveler."

"With your kind hospitality, it's my pleasure."

"Well, thank you. Don't spoil me too much, or I will expect you to come back every time it snows."

Jack shook his head. "Noted." He looked up, connecting to her, eye to eye, and gave her a warm smile. "I'm sorry for falling asleep on the couch last night."

"When you are done, meet me in the kitchen, I am going to whip us up something to eat. Since you didn't get your eggs last night."

"I have to try and get back to my dad at some point. But, I'll come in for a few."

Addison didn't love hearing that he had to leave. If she was honest, she enjoyed having him stay with her. She liked the company.

"Okay."

Addison closed the window and got dressed. She stopped her feelings from controlling her and pushed them down. Sometimes it felt like Jack was straightforward and hinting towards more, and sometimes he was hard to read, hinting towards friendship, leaving her in the dark. Regardless, watching him shovel the driveway reminded her of her dad. She used to wake up early on winter mornings and look out the window, just the same, excited to talk to him. It felt very de ja vu like.

Going downstairs, Addison took out bowls, baking pans, and ingredients. She started chopping veggies and meat and cracked some eggs. Throwing it all together in a glass dish, she placed it on the top tray of the oven and set a timer. Separately, she put flour, blueberries, sugar, vanilla,

117

and oil in a mixer. Then, she poured the mixture into a tin tray, placed it in the second oven, and began baking.

Waiting for Jack, she set out plates, napkins, cutlery, and cups. She brewed a fresh pot of coffee and made freshly squeezed orange juice, setting out a carafe. As the timer on the oven dinged, Jack walked in from the garage.

"Just in time. Breakfast is done. I made muffins and a soufflé."

Jack put his winter stuff to the side, hanging it on a laundry rack to dry. He made his way to the kitchen table and sat down. His cheeks were bright red from the cold. "Feels nice and warm in here."

"Good. Get cozy."

Addison pulled out the tin tray from the oven, showing its golden-brown top, bursting with blueberries and sugar crystals. Then, she opened the other oven and pulled out the soufflé with its golden yellow top. As she cut into the egg to make sure it was done, the steam hit her face. Specks of red and green peppers, slices of ham, and buttered spinach let off a strong aroma, making her stomach growl. Putting a slice on a plate and placing a muffin on the side, she carried the plate to the table and placed it in front of Jack. "Would you like some orange juice?"

"Wow. I could get used to this." Jack winked at her.

"Well, don't be too picky. I'm not a professional."

"It looks perfect."

"How did you sleep last night?" she asked.

"Good, actually," Jack said.

"I'm glad to hear it. The guesthouse is open, whenever you need it. You are an easy house guest."

"I'm sorry, you put all that stuff in there, and I didn't use any of it. All that for nothing."

"Don't be silly. I enjoyed having company. You know, last night was the first time this place felt like a home again. It was the first time I left my bedroom door open."

"I'm glad you had a good night's rest."

"Well, what are you going to do the rest of the day?" Addison asked.

"I'm just hoping my dad is doing okay. Hopefully the heat is still working. I have to go shovel his driveway."

Addison sighed. "I feel awful now. You shouldn't have done mine."

"Don't keep saying that. I wanted to do it."

Addison smiled. "I appreciate it."

As Jack finished up his meal, he looked anxious to get going.

"Jack, before you get going, I just want to say … yesterday was one of the best days since I have been here. I'm not sure I would have gotten through it as easily."

"You are a lot stronger than you give yourself credit for. I didn't do anything."

"If only you knew."

Jack smiled. "Addison, there's something I have been wanting to talk to you about."

"Okay, what is it?"

Jack looked at her. The way she stared at him, the way she saw him, the way she trusted him. It was a glimpse into her heart that he hadn't seen before. She was letting him in. He didn't want to say anything that might change that. He re-thought it and took a sip of his orange juice. "I just wanted to tell you that if you have nowhere to go for Christmas, you are welcome to celebrate with us ... or with me, I should say."

Addison could sense that maybe he wanted to say more but didn't. "Aunt Wanda invited me over for Christmas Eve. I don't have any other plans. I will see how I feel. I'm hoping I don't get bombarded with emotions. Thank you, though. I love the offer."

"Sure." Jack stood up, took his stuff off the drying rack, and went to the door, putting his stuff back on. "I'll hopefully see you around?"

"Yeah, for sure."

Addison wasn't sure when she would see him next, but she was hoping it was sooner than later.

"The weather is supposed to get bad again later. Maybe stay close to home so this guy doesn't worry about you."

"You would worry about me?"

Jack grinned. "We know from last night how unpredictable the weather can be. Just be safe."

Addison smiled. "I will."

Turning to leave, Jack opened the door and walked out. He had to walk back into town and get his car. Addison hated how she felt inside as she watched him go. She was starting to realize that her feelings were much deeper than she realized. She was attached, with a care and concern for him that went well beyond friends. Running up to the loft, she looked out the window and watched him walk through town, thinking over the night before. It made her smile and filled her with happiness.

Addison cleared the dishes, washed up, and went into the family room. Turning on the tv, a frown formed on her face. At the bottom of the screen was a blizzard warning. Another potential whiteout. "Looks like I won't be going anywhere today," she said aloud. Bored and lonely, she began shuffling through things that were hidden away in the basement and hall closet. It helped keep her mind distracted, not knowing how to sort out her feelings over Jack. Another organization job she wasn't thrilled with. But Martha was supposed to come by and get it ready for sale by the end of the week, so she wanted it to be ready.

Addison opened box after box, sifting through memories. She sat on the floor, smiling, laughing, and crying. So many pictures and mementos from her childhood. Picking up a picture of her with both of her parents, she placed it aside to keep. It made her feel good to see the three of them together. The grief and sadness hadn't dissipated, but she was able to contain her emotions more and more as the days went by. She pulled out a large rectangular bin and opened it up. The contents were all Christmas related. Pulling out long strands of garland, toy soldiers, stuffed snowmen, village figurines, and boxes of ornaments, Addison felt chipper, thinking of the last time they decorated the house and tree together. She went into full-on Christmas mode. Pulling out a few things that she had bought at the store as gifts, she grabbed the wrapping paper and went back into the family room. Resting next to the couch, on the floor, while listening to music at a higher volume, she wrapped each item in poinsettia -patterned paper and adhered spiral-like gold ribbons around them. After all of them were finished, she got up and placed them by the fireplace. It wasn't a full Christmas affair like her mom did, but it brought a sense of jolliness to the house.

Addison recited a song out loud. "Oh, the weather outside is frightful, but the fire is so delightful." It ran through Addison's head as she peeked out the window and around the curtains to see four more inches of snow. This time, the weatherman wasn't wrong. It was coming down fast, and it wasn't stopping any time soon. "Err," she huffed.

Going into the kitchen, she grabbed a cup from the cupboard, set it down, and then began brewing hot water for cocoa. Pouring the contents into her cup, chocolate swirled around with frothy whipped cream. Perfect mini squares of marshmallow adorned the top, filling her red ceramic mug that had a knitted sleeve. It was her Christmas mug; a tradition in their household on cold nights that they enjoyed together while watching old movies and sitting by the fire. Taking it with her, she went up to the loft and peeked out the highest window, watching the tree in the downtown square turn on. Its illuminance upon the buildings, homes, and streets made everything look enchanting, like the village was coming alive. She was going to miss it here. She wanted to capture each detail and lock it away in her memory in case she never returned. Looking below, she admired the snowcapped evergreens that lined the house. Everything was glistening, covered with sparkling icy crystals. The shoveled and salted walkways were covered in a light frost. "Winter Wonderland" came on the radio, filling her with joyous memories of Christmases past. Her parents used to dance together, right where she was standing, by the window, looking out at the wonderful panorama of Edgerton. Addison started to hum along with the lyrics and smiled, thinking of them. Then, she went back downstairs to continue her decorating. She pulled out garland from the ornament box, adorning the fireplace mantle. Setting her cup down on the table, she bounced back and forth to the rhythm, enjoying the jolly feeling it left within her.

As she grew tired of sifting through things and she began to get hungry, Addison searched her mom's recipe cards. Searching for ingredients and finding the necessary cooking utensils, Addison set everything out on the counter as she prepared. One by one, she measured things out. Finishing her dough and putting the final touches on her home-made frosting, she set out two pans. One for cinnamon cookies and one for pie. Setting them in the oven, she smiled and walked away. As she headed back into the other room, the ding of the doorbell surprised her, and she jumped. Startled, she stopped for a brief moment and put her hand over her heart. Taking a deep breath, she walked to the door and peeked through the glass to see who it was. Jack, handsome as ever, was standing there, covered in snow and shivering.

Addison opened the door. "Jack, what are you doing back here so soon?"

"I left this morning, and something didn't feel right. I couldn't leave you without making sure you had a tree for Christmas."

Addison gave him a side glance. "What?"

As he moved to the side to show her, there was a medium sized tree behind him. "It was the best one they had for the size."

"You really did that? I can't believe it."

"May I bring it in? There's already enough snow on it."

"Oh, yeah, excuse me. I'm sorry for being rude. Come in."

Jack came forward. But before she let him in completely, Addison stepped forward and hugged him. She couldn't help it. "I need to give you a hug. Thank you. This is incredibly sweet. What a kind gesture. This might be the nicest thing anyone has ever done for me."

"It's nothing. Just something little."

"I wasn't sure that I wanted to see Christmas in this house, knowing I had no one to share it with."

"Sometimes it isn't about that, sometimes it's about the spirit of it. You may not have the people you want, but it will spark joy. It will make you feel happy. You need more happy in your life right now."

Jack entered the house, found a spot in the family room to place the tree stand, and put the tree in its perspective place in the corner. He brushed off the snow as best as he could and dried up the surrounding area with a towel that he brought with.

Addison took out a box of decorations and opened it. "What looks better together, green and gold ornaments or red and gold? And, what kind of lights would look good on the tree? I like white, but some people like colored. What's your preference?" She questioned.

"I like everything," he answered. "Not that I have any say in the matter."

"I enjoy your opinion. You are the one that brought it to me."

Jack turned to leave. "Well, I just wanted to stop and give that to you. I hope it brightens your day."

"Jack, would you stay and help me?" Addison handed him his own box of ornaments, hoping he would say yes.

Jack turned toward her. "If you really want me to, sure."

"I would like the company. Unless you have somewhere to be or someone to be with?"

Addison was lightly prodding him to see his reaction.

"The only person I have to see tonight is you. Otherwise, I have a heifer in heat to check on. But, she can wait till the morning." Jack walked up to the tree and started adding ornaments, one by one.

"I don't want to stand in the way of you and your cows."

"Her name is Daisy. She is one beautiful girl."

"Jack, do you remember how you mentioned that I could come out to your dad's property?"

"Yeah."

"I think I would like to do that before I leave Edgerton."

"Of course. Most of it has been covered by snow, but it's beautiful, nonetheless. You can see my dad's horses and chickens, and I can show you some of his award-winning cows. Oh, that reminds me, I brought you eggs. I set them on the porch. They have to be washed."

"Aww, thank you. Who tends to them when you are back at home in Waterford, seeing that your dad isn't feeling the best lately?"

"We have a family friend, Harry. Harry and his son live down the road. They help out. I pay them when I need to if Dad can't attend to their needs."

"Has he thought of getting rid of some of his animals, knowing he can't take care of them?"

"We've discussed many things. He is stubborn. If it was up to him, he would like me to move here. He says that the property will be mine one day anyway, but I am not one hundred percent comfortable with that. I don't like when he talks like that."

"Can you move? Are you able to?"

"Yeah, of course. It would take more travel on my part, and I would have to transition the office, but I would be able to do it."

"Jack, I hope you don't mind me asking, but do you want to stay in Waterford?"

"Like I said yesterday, I want everything to happen naturally. I am not set in stone with anything. I love where I live. I love my business. I love the people. I'm happy. The only thing I want is a family. I am ready for more. I am ready to start my life with a partner and have kids. I think that's the next step. I want to watch them grow up. I want a safe and peaceful home. I want to cook for someone. I want to build things. I want lots of animals. I want to start my own garden ... but to say where that will be, it depends on the person I end up with. We would both need to compromise and find a place that works for the both of us. If she didn't like Waterford, I would move."

Addison was intrigued. She wasn't used to a sensitive, open, and self-assured man that wasn't afraid to commit. He didn't play games. He was honest about what he wanted. He was up-front, kind, soft-hearted, and patient. He was willing to conform for someone. He was a true catch. From what she knew of him, he had characteristics that were rare in comparison to the men she was used to. His interests were organic and earthy. He was so humble and grounded. Addison felt intimidated by his confidence. He knew who he was and what he wanted. His intentions were pure. He wasn't wrapped up in unnecessary things. He didn't have unrealistic wants. He wanted simple things.

"How about you?" he asked.

"Everything I have ever thought that I wanted, I am second guessing now. I'm starting to feel like it's all fantasy thinking. It's a façade to prove something about myself. Maybe I dreamt those things because I have never really known what I wanted. I don't know what I am supposed to be doing. I don't know what fills me up. You have me thinking."

"Has there ever been a time where you were doing something, and your whole body was energized? You felt so much excitement over it?"

"I don't know."

"You'll know when something is right, and it's meant to be; you will know. There's no way to ignore it, and your heart and mind can't go without it."

Addison was envious of him. His awareness towards all things was inspiring. His character was, by far, the best thing about him, and the more she knew him, the more attracted to him she became. It was a bit unnerving. Maybe he was what she was looking for? Her Mr. Nice guy. But of all the places, why here? And of all the times, why now? She was grieving, and she didn't know if it was the right time to trust her feelings.

As Addison added ornaments to the tree, Jack looked around the family room, picking up a frame with a photo of her mom.

Addison noticed him looking it over. "That's Mom."

"Beautiful. I can see where you get your beauty."

Addison blushed. "She was timeless, just like her antiques. She had this air about her. She was simple yet classy. I actually have a bunch of pictures in a pile over there. I pulled them out today. Would you like to see some?" Addison pulled down a shoebox from atop the piano and opened the lid to show Jack.

"Yeah, that would be great." Jack knew it would mean a lot to her if he looked them over.

Addison put the box in Jack's hands. He sifted through a few of them and then came upon the one of Addison with her parents. "This is a good picture. You must have been eight or nine? You definitely look like your mom, but I can see traits that resemble your dad. You definitely have his nose."

"Yeah. Everyone says that. I have a lot of his personality too."

"Tell me about him. What was he like?"

"He was a go-getter, an organized person, and a stubborn but kind man. He had a sense of humor that was so witty, he had a comeback for everything. He was fun. He had a young spirit. He was an adventure seeker. He liked fixing old cars. He didn't like to travel much away from here, but he enjoyed fast things. He was a busy body. A simple man. He was a realist."

Jack smiled. "He sounds special."

Addison looked at Jack and smiled. "Yeah, he was."

"You have told me a lot about your mom, but what was she like when your dad was around?"

"She was calm, patient, funny, and loving. She was a caretaker. It filled her up to see others happy."

"You are lucky."

Addison looked at Jack, feeling bad that she hadn't asked him about his mom. "I'm sorry, I'm being rude again. Tell me about your mom."

Jack smiled. "She never missed a game of mine. I was a big-time athlete growing up. I played just about everything. She was always there. She was my biggest supporter. She and my dad argued over silly stuff, but overall, I knew they loved one another, and they loved me. I didn't realize how much he needed her until she was gone."

"Do you think your dad is depressed? Maybe he isn't over the loss of her. Even if it's been awhile, some people never move forward. They are stuck in that place."

"No … I … um …"

As Jack tried to get his words out to tell her something, the oven beeper went off. Addison jumped up. "Oh, I forgot. The food."

Jack swallowed and rolled his eyes, frustrated that something always came up when he started to get emotional and connect with her. He took a whiff as the house filled with sweet scents of oven baked goods. "That smells amazing. What did you bake?"

The aroma of boysenberry pie and gingersnaps filled the house. Addison smiled and took them out of the oven, placing them on black iron trivets. "They might not be as good as Bob Costello's, but the attempt is what counts." Circular biscuits made of cinnamon, molasses, powdered ginger, and clove were baked perfectly upon the Teflon sheet pan. Addison took a bite to check the consistency. Their sparkling sugar exterior, crisp edge, and slightly chewy center melted in her mouth. "I don't know, this might be one of my best baking creations. Bob might have competition."

"I must try them, then." Jack walked into the kitchen and took one from the tray. As he placed it in his mouth, he moaned. "Mmm ... I have to agree. Watch out, Bob."

"I made a frosting just in case you want to top it. But that's not all. Look at my pie."

Jack looked at the golden-brown dough that was in a lattice pattern, mixed with dark blue and red fruit-filled filling. "That's a good buttery crust."

"It's my mom's recipe. I figured I'd try it."

Jack cut a slice, took his fork, and put it in his mouth. "Mmm ... it's a tie. Both are equally good. You have impressed me."

"I don't cook that often. It felt nice."

"Why do you think you don't cook?"

"I hate cleaning up afterwards."

Jack laughed. "Is that it?"

"I don't have anyone to cook for either. I guess that would be nice to have."

"Well, if you ever need someone to try out your creations, I will volunteer."

Addison blushed. "Noted." *Maybe he does like me. Maybe this is more than friendly and flirty banter?*

Feeling a bit shy from his kind remarks, Addison looked away, straightening up the kitchen. She had never felt so self-conscious in someone's presence before. He made her so fidgety and so alive with energy, she lost her train of thought. She wanted him to think highly of her. He was such a good person and had so much going for him, it made her question whether or not she was good enough.

Jack sensed her discomfort. "Addison, thank you. It has been so nice having you around and spending time together. I'm glad I walked into the store that day. I'm glad that we met. I appreciate your friendship."

Addison tried digesting exactly what he was saying. Was this the friendzone speech? Was this goodbye? Had she been reading the signs wrong? This was what she was afraid of and why she didn't make a move.

She looked at him and nodded her head, agreeing with him. "I agree. It has been really nice."

"I appreciate your hospitality, but I should probably get going."

"Oh. Okay. Sure."

As Jack went to walk through the hallway, the lights flickered.

"Uh, what was that?" Addison asked with fear in her voice.

"It might be the electricity. It's windy, and we are getting so much snow."

"Oh, gosh. I won't be able to sleep tonight. I hate when it's pitch black. Especially in this big house."

"Would you like me to stay a little longer to make sure?"

Just then, the lights went out. It was dark. Addison began to freak out. "Oh, no, oh, no, oh, no." She jumped.

Jack walked over to her and reached for her hand. "Give me your hand. I will walk you to the couch and then I'll find some candles."

"What would I do without you?" Taking Jack's hand, Addison felt safe. She squeezed it.

He helped her over to the couch, and she sat there, waiting for him to find a light source.

"Where do you normally keep matches or lighters?" Jack asked.

"In the cabinet next to the oven," Addison said.

Jack went to the cabinet and fiddled around. He pulled out a box of matches and walked over by the sink where he knew a candle was sitting. He took the top off and lit it. "We have light."

Addison smiled. She stared at her hand, wishing his was still upon it. She was so glad he stayed. She didn't like admitting it, but she relied on his instinct and sensibility. He walked over to the couch and set the candle down on the table beside them. Sitting next to Addison, he looked at her endearingly. He had a natural desire to take care of her. They were close to one another, forming a sense of intimacy, sharing stories and opening their hearts.

Addison looked at Jack and then felt sad. "Jack, I'm going back to New York soon. I'm just here for another few days. I don't know how I will say goodbye to this house or you. It's going to be difficult."

"Why don't you stay for the new year?"

Addison immediately thought about her commitment with Greyson and was less than thrilled. "I can't. I have plans. I already committed to going to dinner with one of my bosses. He asked me to be on the next ad campaign with him. I know it sounds bad that I have to go to dinner with him in order to get the job, but he's just that type of guy; very ego-driven."

Jack had a hard time hearing her say that. "Lucky guy."

"It's not like that."

"Are you sure he thinks that?"

"I don't know, but I'm going to make sure he knows. I have hinted towards it. I'm not looking forward to it."

"Don't get yourself in a bind that you can't escape from. Some men don't take no for an answer."

"What does that mean?"

"It's just, I can tell by the way he asked you out, setting it up before you work together, that he's arrogant, and he expects to get his way."

"You are probably right. He's definitely a narcissist, and he is very persistent."

"Don't give him what he wants then. He's expecting the date to solidify something romantically. I can almost promise you that he likes you beyond a business partner. Unless that is what you want and what you are looking for?"

"I wasn't planning on letting it go anywhere. I'm not interested in that way. Give me more credit than that. However, there are random moments where he surprises me, and I think for a brief moment that he could be a good guy, and I see a glimpse of this decent, charming person."

That comment irked Jack, and he became antsy and uncomfortable. "Well, it's your decision."

"I don't know if I will ever get this opportunity again."

"To have your face and body plastered everywhere? To be on billboards and in magazines? If that's what you want, that's great."

"I don't know. It sounds fun and adventurous, and I know it will lead to job security and a different pay scale. I could use a good change."

"It's all about what makes you happy. But if I can give you advice from a man that's a tad older and a bit more settled than you … don't focus on the money. Focus on where your heart takes you; the money will follow. You don't seem to gravitate towards a lot of 'in your face' stuff. So, I just don't want you to regret it. Once you are out there, you are out there. You can't take your face off those billboards. Everyone will be in your business. No more privacy."

"I guess I won't know until I try."

"Have you ever thought about staying here, getting away from the hustle and bustle and reconnecting to your younger self, seeing it in a new light?"

"Up until now, no. I have too much curiosity. I will admit, this has been a great visit. I have a new appreciation for Edgerton. I have felt so relaxed here. Everyone is so friendly, so nice. It's peaceful. There have been a few moments that stopped me in my tracks to think about it, but nothing strong enough that would draw me to stay." Addison knew the only thing that could possibly get her to reconsider was Jack asking her. But he didn't seem willing or ready for that, based on their current conversation.

Jack shook his head slowly, looking displaced. "Hmm ... well, everything will work out the way it's supposed to. I want nothing but the best for you."

He became removed and distant. He was bothered by her lack of connection to him. He thought they were building something. She dismissed it, as if it wasn't even a mere thought in contemplation as to her future and what they might be together. He began thinking it over. Was it a lack of communication? Was he making her feel that way? Looking at her, stunning as ever, he questioned himself. Why would she want to leave her exciting life in New York for him? He was too normal and plain. He was a country boy; he lived the life that she was trying so desperately to get away from. As badly as he wanted her, he didn't want to limit her. He had thought of making a move and kissing her so many times, but he was old-fashioned. He liked taking things slow and building the foundation before getting intimate. He knew from past relationships that intimacy had a tendency to cloud his judgement, and in effect, he would look past important things just because it felt good. He didn't want that with her. He was looking for the real thing. He didn't want to mess this up. But it dawned on him, in that moment, that maybe by taking things so slow, he had given her the wrong impression. Maybe she needed reassurance?

What just happened, she thought. Why couldn't he just say how he was feeling? She was confused emotionally. Did he like her or didn't he? Clearing her throat, she wanted to make sure he didn't feel offended because of something she said. "If I can be honest, I like when you are around."

Enjoying her comment, Jack swallowed and looked directly at her. "Yeah, me too." Jack smiled, but he was still put off by her comments about the future. It didn't fit with his life, and he knew his feelings for her needed to go to the wayside. He couldn't and wouldn't try to change her.

Wanting to switch subjects to remove the awkwardness, Jack started humming a Christmas melody. "I should try calling my dad. If the power is out here, it's probably out there, too."

Dialing the numbers, Jack anxiously waited for his dad to pick up. "Come on, Dad, pick up." There was no answer. It went to voicemail. "Ugh, he's not picking up. I don't want to leave you in this condition, but I need to check on him. I'm sure the lights will come on in the next hour."

Addison felt disappointed. She didn't want him to leave. Something inside of her longed for more time with him. "Okay. I'll walk you out." Addison carried the candle in her hand, lighting the way.

As they walked to the door, Addison wanted to say so many things. She wanted to tell him that she was interested in him. She wanted to ask him to stay. But she couldn't. She had already missed her chance, and nothing would come out. Her fears crept in. The thought of rejection was too much.

As Jack opened the front door and took a step out, he turned back, looking at Addison one last time. His handsome face under the snow, captured her. She was having a hard time controlling her thoughts. He had an innocence and softness about his face that made him so lovable. There they were, at a crossroads, unable to move forward. Both of them wanted each other, but both were too hesitant and too scared. There was too much standing in their way. Too much that they couldn't make sense of. There wasn't an easy, clear picture as to what their future could be, them wanting opposite lifestyles. There was a disconnect in their communication, creating doubts in both of their minds. As the doubts added up, it was hard for either of them to open up and be vulnerable, professing their true feelings. So they let it be; they let the moment pass, and they continued to long for one another.

"Be sure to stop by," he said.

"I will make time. I hope your dad is okay. And thanks again. This was such a treat."

"No problem. Good to see you again. Bye."

Addison shut the door behind him and closed her eyes. She had a wonderful man right in front of her, and she was ruining it. She was letting him get away. Addison walked back to the couch and laid down, letting her mind rest. She placed the candle on the table and closed her eyes. Slowly, without thought, she fell into a light slumber.

Hours later, there was a knock at the door. Addison grew nervous, seeing that it was close to midnight. She woke up out of her sleep, groggy and out of sorts. The lights were back on. She blew out the candle and went towards the front door. Opening it, she sighed happily. She was surprised but not shocked.

"You are back so soon," Addison said. She rubbed her eyes and yawned.

Jack had his hands in his pockets. His breath was sifting through the cold air. "I'm sorry. Did I wake you? I couldn't help it. I had to check on you. I couldn't go to sleep until I knew you were okay, and your electricity came back on."

"I think we should exchange cell phone numbers. It would have been much easier to text or call me. I am so sorry you did that. I just woke up. I must have fallen asleep. They seem to be back on. How about your dad? Did he lose power?"

"No. He fell asleep, and that's why he didn't answer. He was fine."

"So, you drove all the way back to your dad's and all the way back here? Why would you do that? That is so selfless of you."

"I couldn't relax. I was picturing you in my head sitting in this big house with one candle, scared and cold."

"First of all, do I give off that helpless vibe? If so, that's not a good look. I need to work on that. And I was fine. I have blankets. I just curled up on the couch and dozed off."

"I'm glad you were able to sleep so easily. I didn't mean that you seemed helpless, just that you weren't used to being in this type of situation; in this house with this weather."

"Jack, you keep on surprising me. Do you ever do anything for you? You are always doing everything to take care of everyone else."

"I wouldn't say checking on you is just for you. I get the perks of seeing you."

Addison blushed. "You just like my cooking."

"Is it breakfast time yet?" Jack joked.

Addison laughed. "You can stay. Guest house is always open."

"No. I'm going to go. I just wanted to see you, so I could relax. Now that I have, I will stop bugging you."

"You would never bug me. Seeing you is the highlight of my days here."

Jack shook his head and smiled. It was a silent, awkward moment. They were in a place where no one knew what to say. Jack desperately wanted her, but there was something he still hadn't told her. He couldn't move forward without divulging it and discussing it. He just didn't know how to bring it up. Every time he tried, something came up or stopped him.

Breaking up the moment, knowing nothing was going to change, Addison yawned again. "Well, I'll see you soon, then?"

Jack, knowing the moment was lost, felt defeated. He had this beautiful, well-put together, amazing, intelligent, and funny woman standing in front of him, and he was ruining it. He was letting her go, and he didn't know how to rectify it. The longer he went without telling her and without making a move, he was pushing her further away. He wanted to tell her all the things he liked about her; he wanted to kiss her; he wanted to sweep her up in his arms and cuddle with her. He wanted to push reason and fear aside and enjoy the moment. He took a deep breath and swallowed, feeling overwhelmed, trying to think of the right thing to say.

"Addison, please know, just because I don't say something doesn't mean I don't feel it."

Addison thought about what he was saying. What did that mean exactly? Being late at night and not wanting to dissect it, making it more awkward, she nodded her head to let him know that she understood. "Okay, Jack, drive safe."

As the door closed, once again, they were in the same place. Stuck somewhere between friends and flirty banter.

Chapter 7: Winter Surprise

The next morning, Addison peeked out her window as the sun started to rise. She fixated her eyes down below, next to her oak tree. There, rested the most perfectly sculpted snowman. And written in the snow were the words, "have a good day." Addison, instantaneously smiling, knew who did it. Feeling like a kid inside, she ran down the stairs, threw on a coat and boots, and went outside to get an up-close view. As she got closer, something stood out and made her chuckle. Not only did the snowman have a black top hat, corn cob pipe, carrot nose, and button-down front, but affixed around the neck was a little piece of plaid fabric. Their joking term, team plaid, played through her head, bringing her back to the day they met. Addison looked to her right and noticed something placed in the newspaper mailbox tube. Walking a few feet to retrieve it, she took it in her hands and looked it over. It was a note with her name on it. He had placed it in hard plastic wrapping, so it didn't get wet. She shook it a few times to get the remnants of snow and debris off of it. Walking back into the house, she unraveled the plastic, undoing the top adhesive, pulling out the note to read the contents.

Addison,

Meet me in Town Square, 12:00 noon. Off Jefferson Street.

Yours Truly,

Jack

Addison scrunched her forehead thinking about what this entailed. What could he possibly be up to? And was she up for it? The excitement and anticipation had her feeling very fidgety. She went into the kitchen, set the note down, started a pot of coffee, and made some toast. She was daydreaming as she spread the butter and jam across her bread. Was he taking her on a date? What was this? Should she dress up, or should she be casual? Would they be inside or outside? So many variables to think about. She brought her food and drink into the family room and turned the tv on. Listening to the television, she calmed down for the slightest bit and then nerves billowed right back up, leaving her unable to sit still. The restless energy in her legs made it difficult to stay in one place. Leaving her stuff on the coffee table, she went upstairs and started pulling out clothes. Shirt by shirt, she laid them out on her bed. Starting the shower, she waited for it to get hot and steamy before getting in. Addison hummed songs and allowed the good feelings to take over her mood. She whistled the tunes of her favorite Christmas songs. For a brief second, as she got to "Jingle Bell Rock," she had a flashback to the office Christmas party. Quickly, she changed her frame of thought and energy to a more playful tune. "Frosty the Snowman" seemed fitting. She loved the youthful vibe that the morning presented. It made her feel rejuvenated and got her mind off of everything with the store and house. Addison took her time getting ready, allowing time to pass, getting her closer to twelve o'clock. As she styled her hair and put on her make-up, she looked in the mirror. "I have to say, you look pretty good, Ms. Monroe," she said out loud to herself. Then, she chuckled at herself for being so corny and self-amused.

As she looked at the clock, she scrambled to get her coat, hat, gloves, shoes, and scarf on. It was a shame to put a hat over her smooth blown-out hair, but she wasn't sure what they were doing, and it was quite brisk out. Closing up, she made her way to the cobblestone walkway, heading into town. It was a gorgeous day with the sun fully shining, the snow sparkling, and the trees covered. She couldn't wipe the smile off her face. As she walked to Main Street, Addison couldn't help herself. She found herself waving and saying hello to everyone that she saw. What was happening to her? This town had an enchanted spell over her. She was turning into a chipper, overly-friendly townie, just like the people that normally annoyed her. She had to admit, it felt nice. Expression, connection, relationships; it was bringing out a side of her that she hadn't allowed out in a very long time. It made her vulnerable, open, and spirited.

Following the path to Jefferson, she looked for any sign of Jack. She kept her eyes peeled to both sides of the street. As she came to the crosswalk and went to turn the corner, she saw him. Standing in front of a large ice rink with skates in his hands, Jack awaited her with a smile. Fixating her eyes on his, she instantaneously grew butterflies in her stomach, while also feeling a sense of comfort and belonging. His smile lit up his face, and it put her at ease.

"Well, hello. Aren't you full of surprises," she said.

"I never get to do this. I thought it would be fun. It's not Rockefeller Center, but it's the two of us, and to me, that seemed good enough a reason. It's not about the location; it's about the people you are with, right?"

Addison shook her head yes, while keeping a bashful grin on her face. "Yeah." She didn't want to admit it, but in that moment, she fell for him just a little bit more. His charm had an effect on her. She was a bit entranced and enamored by him. Maybe it was the sweetness in his gestures; maybe it was the smoothness to his voice; maybe it was the confidence in his being; maybe it was the way he looked at her and made her feel while being in his presence. Whatever it was, it was working. He was slowly captivating her and pulling her in, getting her to drop her guard.

"By the way, thank you for building the snowman. That was nice," she said while slightly giggling.

"Everyone has to have a tree, and everyone has to have a snowman. The rules of country life. No, actually, those are the rules of winter."

Addison laughed. "I thought that only applied in our early adolescent years?"

"Nope. That's the problem. Everyone grows up and forgets how to enjoy life. You can't stop living just because you are older. There are plenty of ways to have fun and still enjoy the things of our childhood as adults." Jack put his hand out, allowing Addison to grab hold of it, leading her down the walkway to where he was standing. He handed her the skates. "Well, shall we?"

Taking the skates to a bench and changing into them, she watched as people skated around the rink. "I need to warn you, I might fall. I haven't done this in a long time."

"That's okay. I might too. This doctor may need a doctor."

Addison clenched her teeth. "Let's hope not."

He had a way of making everything seem okay. He was reassuring and not much fazed him. She didn't have to put on an act to impress him. He wasn't looking for perfection; he just wanted her to be herself, to be real, to live in the moment, to experience something new. He liked her just the way she was, and that, in itself, made her adore him.

As they made their way to the ice, slowly gliding their feet, one by one, Addison put her hands out to keep balance.

Jack looked at her and smiled. "Do you need a hand?"

"Umm ... I don't remember it being this difficult just to stand up on them. Maybe it's the skates? My ankles are wobbly."

"You will get used to it. Do you want one of those skater aids, it's like a push cart, walker, type thing?"

"The ones they use for toddlers?" Addison opened her mouth and gasped. "Absolutely not." She was bound and determined with gusto and stubbornness. She was not going to be embarrassed or need one of those. Pushing her arms out for strength, she went onto the ice and began moving forward. She didn't want to look at Jack. She was trying to concentrate. But as she started to get going, a little kid came whizzing by her, frightening her. She tensed up, hit a tiny nick in the ice and felt herself lunging forward, going down face first. As she closed her eyes, afraid of hitting the cold ice, she felt the soft touch of Jack. His warmth, his arms, his strength, it embraced her and wrapped her up safely, catching her. As he turned her forward, he swiped the frost from her coat and face and swiped her hair out of her eyes.

"Are you okay?" he asked.

Opening her eyes, she was completely mortified. "Mm-hmm."

She didn't know if it was the adrenaline or a momentary feeling of relief that came over her, but as she looked into his eyes, she thought one thing. How could anyone be as perfect as him? He was like her knight in shining armor, always there to save her and protect her. Even though she didn't need anyone to take care of her, it felt nice. She hadn't felt that kind of care from a man ever, besides from her dad. As she grew stable on her feet, and he backed away a tiny bit, he chuckled. "You sure did try. I gotta say, for a mere second, I thought you were going to show me up and throw out some moves. Those arms were flailing, and you were concentrating hard."

Addison couldn't help it. She started laughing. She had to laugh at herself. She must have looked ridiculous. "I'm such a dork."

"No, you are perfect."

As the words escaped his mouth, Addison gulped and caught her breath. It took her back.

Jack didn't give her time to reply, he started skating around her, backwards, forwards, in a circle. He was showing off.

Her mouth dropped open. Everything about him was attractive, as he exuded confidence. "I thought you said you didn't get to do this often. It looks like you do this a lot."

"I play hockey."

"What? No fair. Why didn't you tell me that before I tried to be all cool and skate first?"

"I didn't want you to overthink it."

Addison bit her bottom lip, smirked, and playfully shook her head at him. "You got me."

Jack skated next to her as she continued to struggle. "Are you sure you don't want the skater aid until you get more comfortable? Don't feel weird about it. I don't care."

Addison thought about wiping out again. "Yeah, I will try it for a bit."

Jack went over to grab it and then slid it in front of her. Slowly, they skated together around the edge.

"It's beautiful out today," Addison said.

Jack looked at her. "Yeah, it is." After a few minutes of silence, Jack cleared his throat. She could tell he had something on his mind. "Can I admit something?"

Afraid of what he might say, she furrowed her brows and bit the inside of her cheek. "Umm … sure."

"I missed you. I know that might sound funny since I just saw you, but every time I have to leave you, it's like a part of me just misses being around you. I enjoy being with you and spending time together. When I go home, I think about the next time I might get to talk to you or see you again."

It filled her up, hearing affirmation of his feelings. It wasn't all in her head. Addison's eyes grew wide, and she sucked in her lips. He was being so vulnerable. She felt the same, but it scared her thinking of having to go back to New York so soon. She smiled, acknowledging his kind remarks. "I'm glad I got to see you today."

"Any chance you want to hang out again tomorrow for a little bit? I have somewhere I want to take you."

"Yeah, I'd like that. I have plans in the afternoon and early evening, but I could work around it."

"Great. I will pick you up. If I can take a few of your morning hours, I will have you back in time."

"Perfect." As Addison filled up with happiness, she let go of the push cart. She was skating steady without it. She was feeling light and free.

Her body was loose, and she let the air hit her face as she moved briskly across the rink.

With each conversation, with each meeting, with each new moment together, Addison thought about what kept her feeling so attached to him. They connected equally on so many levels. Their energy met in a synchronized fashion. There was consistency in his actions and behaviors. His conversation had more depth and feeling than most men her age. He was willing to put it all out there; he was willing to talk freely without worry. The connection was on a different level, something that reached spiritually, mentally, and emotionally. It was easy to joke around, but it was also easy to discuss the difficult issues of the world and listen to each other's views, respecting one another, something that was very rare to find. As they learned about one another, opening themselves up more and more, it created a sense of trust and a bond that felt sacred. It was deeper than a friendship. It was soulful.

Jack playfully danced to the town music that was playing on the Bluetooth speakers as he moved about. Addison rolled her eyes at him. "Oh, boy," she said.

"What? You don't dance? Or you do, but it's only in the shower and in your bedroom?"

"The latter."

"Is it because you are worried about what people might think, or is it because you don't like dancing much?"

"I'm just not comfortable with people staring at me."

"For someone that wants to be on billboards, that doesn't match up."

"They will be staring at a picture of me, not me, specifically."

"Okay, I can understand that. But what if you just let it all go and don't care what anyone thinks? What might happen? They will think you are fun; they will think you are goofy; they will think you are silly; they will want to be like you; they will grow envious. You can't control what people think of you, and they are going to make up their minds one way or another."

"I doubt anyone would be envious of my dance moves."

"Give it a try. I dare you."

"No, I can't."

"Oh, yes, you can."

Jack spun around her on his skates and took her hand in his, slowly moving her around in a circle, making sure she didn't fall. He playfully moved her arms in the air and made silly facial gestures at her. She was amused, but still not ready to put herself on display. "How do you do it, Jack?"

"Do what?"

"Just be yourself, without any thought, care, or worry in the world. Don't you have insecurities?"

"Of course, I do. I have many. But people making fun of me, judging me, accepting me, that isn't one of them. If they don't like me for me, then they don't like me. If I have to act like someone else or hide who I really am to be accepted, then they like a version of me, not the real me. I am a good person, and I know that."

"I wish I was like that."

"You can try and control how people perceive you, but it won't stop them from making their own judgements. You are not going to get along with everyone. Some people will love you; some people won't. That's the truth. If you are happy with yourself, if you are your most authentic self, that's all that matters, and you will notice that people tend to gravitate towards that. People like connecting with something real, flaws and all. It makes you more approachable and allows them to meet you where you are at, allowing them to be themselves too."

"Maybe that's why I'm drawn to you."

Jack raised his eyebrows and smirked. "Hmm—I would like to get into this conversation a little more, but it looks like they are pushing us off the ice."

Addison looked to the right and saw everyone exiting. There was a town official maneuvering the crowd to the side. Addison and Jack made their way to him. "Why is this closing, sir?" Jack asked.

"It will open again tonight at eight."

Jack raised his upper lip, showing Addison he was less than thrilled by that answer. Whispering, he mouthed words to her. "I'm sorry, I should have looked at the times better."

Addison smiled and shook her head at him, letting him know that it didn't matter to her. As they sat on the bench and took their skates off, there was an awkward silence. "Jack, this was the kindest, most thoughtful day any man has planned for me. You have made me smile during a time when I thought it was impossible. Thank you so much." She handed him the skates and stood up. "I should get going." Addison knew she was cutting the time short, not allowing for additional conversation. The unknown made her uneasy, wanting to flee. As she went to turn around, he tried connecting to her, eye to eye.

The desire between them was strong, but more than that, the trust and friendship was growing. Jack felt it was as good a time as any to share with her what burdened him. He took a few seconds to organize his thoughts. Swallowing, trying to relieve what felt like a lump in his throat, he re-positioned himself. Pulling nervously on his bottom lip, contemplating the worst scenario and outcome from what he had to tell her, he began to speak. "So …"

She was flustered, sensing he was nervous. She stood up, ignoring that he was about to say something. "See you tomorrow," she said.

A bit disappointed, but not put off, knowing she needed more time, Jack dropped his shoulders, kindly smiled, and accepted the little time they had. He had this guilt residing within him that he needed to get off his chest. The longer he waited, the harder it was to confide in her about it. And the more he liked her, the more nervous he became. He wanted to get it off his chest and be open. Maybe she could sense that he was holding something back. Maybe she knew he was trying to tell her something. Maybe that's why there was always an interruption. Maybe she didn't want to know.

Standing up, he put his hands in his coat pockets and gave her a soft smile. "Yep, see you tomorrow," he said, letting his words echo behind her. He sat there watching her walk away. He knew it deep within, she was special. He would do anything to win her over. But he also knew, he was running out of time. He needed to lay all his cards on the table. He needed to be honest. He needed to tell her everything, opening his heart in full.

Chapter 8: A Sweet Adventure

Addison woke up tired. She didn't get much sleep. She tossed and turned all night thinking about Jack. Was she being silly entertaining a flirty friendship? Was it going to break her heart when she had to say goodbye? Was she leading him on, making him think that she would stay? Her heart pulled in one direction, and her head pulled in the other. Trying to conceal the dark under eye circles that appeared upon her face, she finished applying her make-up and got ready to head out. Going downstairs and looking out the window, waiting for Jack to pull up, she took a deep breath in. "Just be cool," she said out loud.

Five minutes later, a vintage, blue and white, 1960's pick-up truck pulled in to the driveway. Addison opened the house entry door and waved. Locking up, she closed it behind her and started walking towards him. She was feeling quite bashful, knowing he was probably staring at her. She glanced up at him. He put his window down. "Good morning."

Addison smiled. "Good morning."

Jack opened his door and got out. Walking around her and meeting her by the passenger side door, he opened it for her. Addison enjoyed his chivalry and gentlemanly ways. "Thank you," she said, pulling herself up onto the seat. Jack shut it and walked back around to his side. As he got in, he looked at her and raised his eyebrows. "First of all, you look great. Second of all, Merry Christmas Eve. Third, hi."

Addison couldn't help but fall for his charm. He had the most infectious personality. Every kind word melted her, more and more. She smiled. "Hi. Thank you. And Merry Christmas Eve."

Jack reversed out of the driveway and put it in drive. "Ready?"

"Yeah, where to?"

"It's a surprise. A good surprise. I think you are going to love it."

"I liked the last one. If it's anything like that, I will love it."

"It's even better."

Jack and Addison rode twenty minutes west, halfway between Edgerton and Waterford. As Jack pulled in to a secluded forest, he drove back on a narrow, bumpy, snow-covered road.

"Oh, boy. Where are we going?"

Jack didn't answer. He continued driving in mystery until they came to a parking lot. There were lots of lights everywhere. On the trees, on the park buildings, and on the trail signs. He put the truck into park, got out, went and opened Addison's door, and then grabbed a back pack from the tailgate.

"Are we hiking?" she asked.

"Good thing you wore boots."

"I assumed it was something outside."

"It's not hiking. But we do have to trek through the snow to get there. It's through the woods, past these buildings."

"Now I'm scared. Animal sightings?"

"No. No animals. Even though, I wouldn't mind that."

Jack led Addison on a snow path about a half mile past the parking lot. Slowly, before her eyes, appeared a village of igloos. Jack looked at her and winked. "Cool, huh?"

"Wow. This is amazing."

A long row of interconnected igloos, lit up, lining the whole back area. In front, were larger, separate ones. Jack went into one of the larger ones in front and placed his backpack down. Pulling out a large blanket, he laid it on the floor. "I brought you some snow pants, too, just in case you wanted to put them on, so you don't get your clothes wet. Pulling out a pair of winter overalls, he handed them to her. As she put them on, Jack led her outside and into one of the back igloos. As Addison walked in, she was stunned. It had red neon lights, techno holiday dance music, and a small bar set-up. There was a bartender standing to the side. Jack nodded his head at the man, and Addison waved. "Hello," they said.

"Hello," the bartender replied.

On the counter of the bar was one single flower, a candle, and two glow-in-the-dark temperature changing cups filled with sparkling wine. Jack grabbed the flower and held it in front of his body, presenting it to Addison. "This is for you."

Addison took the flower from him and put it up to her nose and smelled it. It didn't have a scent. She looked over its appearance, marveling at the openness of the white and pink petals. "This is beautiful and different. What kind of flower is it?"

"It's called the Christmas rose or better known as a Helleborus."

"I love it."

"I thought you would. When I looked at it, it made me happy. Just like you."

Addison sucked in her lips trying to contain the beaming smile that wanted to present itself. And even though it was cold in the igloo and she was surrounded by ice, she felt warmth. A heat was building up inside of her. Her cheeks were turning cherry red. Grabbing the glass from the bar, she put it up to her lips and took a sip. The bubbles in the wine hit her tongue just right, leaving a light tickle. "Yum, sweet and no bitter aftertaste."

Jack motioned towards his drink, acknowledging that she didn't cheers him. Picking up his glass, he raised it in the air. "To good things ahead."

Addison clinked her glass into his. "I like the sound of that."

Just then, a gruff, low voice interrupted them. "Excuse me, I just wanted to let you know that I'm here to serve you. Please let me know if you would like anything else. This is what was pre-ordered. But we have signature ice shooters, cider, coffee, and water. Ask and you shall receive."

Addison smiled at the man. "Thank you for offering, but I'm good. This is perfect." She looked at Jack. "Actually, I need to be careful. I have somewhere to be, and I didn't eat."

Jack had a grin on his face. "I came prepared. That brings us to our next stop."

Jack led Addison into the next lit up igloo. As they walked in, it was neon green, and in the center was a table of food. The music was reminiscent of the 60's and 70's, playing old vintage holiday hits. Laid out before them was a charcuterie board full of cheese, cut up sausage, fruits, crackers, bruschetta, bread, chicken salad, and veggies.

Addison's eye grew wide. "This looks so good."

"What's your favorite food?" Jack asked her.

"Pizza. Or pasta. Or chicken parmesan. Basically, anything Italian."

"Mine is Mexican food. I probably should have asked you before I ordered all of this, but then it wouldn't have been a surprise."

"I love all of this. It looks wonderful."

"They order it fresh from the deli in town. They have the best stuff in there."

"Oh ... Giovanni's Delicatessen. I love their sandwiches. They have the best homemade chips too. And, the cannoli's are out of this world."

"Oh, you like those?"

"One of my favorites."

Jack was taking notes in his mind. "I like a good old-fashioned chocolate chip cookie."

Addison laughed. "Simple with your life, simple with your food choices, is that about right?"

"I wouldn't say that exactly. I am willing to try just about anything. I've been venturing out more and more, trying new things. I will never turn down a homecooked meal."

"Unless it's mine, maybe. You haven't had an actual meal of mine yet, just baked goods and eggs."

"I have faith in you. I think you can probably cook up a nice meal."

Addison raised her forehead, widened her eyes, and grinned. "You are too nice."

Jack sat down in one of the chairs. "Go ahead and eat. I know you are hungry."

Addison laughed. "I won't eat Aunt Wanda's dinner tonight if I stuff my face here."

"Eat what you want, I will save the rest. I'll have them pack it up for me. It's just me and my dad tonight. I have to run back into town when we get back, just to get a few things for dinner, but he will eat whatever we don't."

"Jack, do you have extended family? Do you have anyone else close by to spend the holidays with?"

"I do. Most of them live by me in Waterford. Dad's not in the mood for company, and I didn't want to push the issue. I think he just needs time. Maybe a bug going around that has him feeling extra tired. I'm sure he will be feeling better soon."

"Usually, I work on Christmas Eve, and then I go home and watch movies until I fall asleep," Addison said.

"By yourself?" Jack asked.

"I know. Boring, right?"

"No. Not if you enjoy that."

"I do, but it does get a little lonely. When I see families gathering together or little kids playing, it makes me miss my family."

"So, Wanda's house will be nice for you, then."

"I guess. I don't know anyone there. I will probably feel out of place. But, I know my mom would be happy that I visited with her."

"That's nice of you."

Addison snacked on a few bites of mozzarella cheese. "I could eat this every day."

"Not to interrupt your moment of bliss with assorted cheeses, but do you think we can talk a bit?"

Addison grew anxious and started to fidget not knowing where the conversation was going. This was the moment she was hoping for, and for some reason, now that it was here, she was growing tense and uncomfortable. Why did she always have to be so backwards and uptight? She swallowed the bite of food that was in her mouth and then sat up straight. "Of course. What's up?"

"I guess I'm just wondering how you are, how you are feeling, what you are thinking about, and overall, I'm curious what's going on in that head of yours ..."

Her throat went dry. She nervously rubbed her lips together and picked at her fingers. "I'm not always good at stating my feelings."

"You said something yesterday before we got off the ice rink and then we didn't get to discuss it."

"Oh, that was nothing. I was just playing around." Addison didn't want to get into an emotional conversation while she was drinking wine. She wanted a clear head. And, she wanted to enjoy their date together without the heaviness of expectations and feelings. It felt so nice to be out of the house, having fun, laughing and not thinking. The last couple weeks were filled with emotional breakdowns and losses. She wanted to ride the high of feeling happy in Jack's presence and not ruin anything. She was so afraid of saying the wrong thing and tarnishing what they have built. She knew she had a tendency to put her foot in her mouth or say things off the cuff and rub people the wrong way. She didn't always have the right words, mis-communicating. Jack meant something to her, and it was so important that they left each other on a good note.

Jack's demeanor changed a bit. He looked confused. He was finally trying to open up and communicate, so there was nothing left unsaid and they didn't have any regrets, but he could feel her pushing back again. Her comment triggered something inside of him that immediately led him to shut down emotionally. It reminded him of his last relationship, getting little to no validation, overthinking, doubting, and constantly being on different wavelengths. He furrowed his brows. "Oh, of course. I should have known." He was disappointed. How could he tell her what he needed to tell her, if she wasn't open to hearing it? It put him in a bad spot.

Addison felt bad for changing the mood. She wanted to see him smile again. "Jack, I danced in the shower, in the living room, and in the kitchen this morning. Your advice is rubbing off on me. You would have been so proud."

Jack forced a laugh trying not to sulk, staying in his feelings. "I am sure that was fun. I did, however, say to venture out a bit. Dance in public next time, see how liberating it feels."

"Okay, I will try it."

"How about now?"

Addison scrunched up the left side of her face. "You want me to dance while I eat?"

"Put the food down. I'll dance with you. It's the oldies. This is good-time music."

Jack got up and started swaying his body. Addison got up and joined in, swaying back and forth to the beat. They both started laughing. Jack joked around and started mimicking signature dance moves such as the Roger Rabbit, Running Man, and Sprinkler. Even though it didn't go with the era of music, Addison joined in, Voguing and doing the Cabbage Patch. They were almost in tears. Their stomach muscles hurt from laughing so hard. They were building up a sweat. Jack put his arm out and Addison grabbed ahold of his hand as it passed near her face. They started twirling each other around. Jack pulled her in, swung her outwards, dipped her, and then let her go. They faced each other and then went down into the Twist. As they got to the ground, Addison had a hard time getting back up. She started giggling, looking at Jack for help. "I am too low."

He raised his eyebrows at her and gave her a mischievous look. "I am older than you, and I got up. You can do it."

She couldn't stop giggling. "It's these big hefty overalls."

Jack leaned down and helped her up. As she calmed down, there was a moment of silence between them. Their eyes connected, fueling their passion for one another. "For the record, this has been the best time I've had in a very long time, and maybe the best outing with a woman … ever."

Addison put her hand on her chest, taken by his words. He was endearing, melting her heart. She smiled at him. "That's so sweet of you to say. Thank you. You have made me feel comfortable and beautiful."

"You are incredibly beautiful, striking really. Every time I look at you, I am in awe a little bit more. And the part I love the most is that you don't even realize how much. I've never been a man with a wandering eye or someone that wished for more. I've always just wanted to find my other half. I want to give her everything. And I'm not saying that to put pressure on you or discuss something that you are not ready for. I just want you to know that if it was up to me, I would take you out again. Again, and again, and again. Every minute I spend with you is a privilege, and I feel honored.

You constantly make sure that I am having a good time and that I am taken care of. I appreciate that."

"You, as well." Addison bit her bottom lip but said nothing else. The sexual pull between them had been so strong, but now it was emotional. It was starting to feel real. A heaviness came over her, she was trying to sort it out, knowing that they were opposites. How could she lead him on and commit herself, knowing they didn't want the same kind of life? On the other hand, she knew she may never find this kind of connection and this caliber of a man ever again. She'd be a fool to let him go. She was trying to enjoy him in the moment and not think ahead. If this was a short-lived, flirty friendship, then she would always remember it as being the best winter fling of her life.

Jack gave her mischievous eyes and then broke up the awkwardness. "There's one more igloo with dessert, but then let's do something fun."

"Like what?"

"Let's sled down that big hill we passed on the way in."

Addison sighed and gave him a side smirk, looking worried. "We don't have sleds, and I don't think it's a sledding hill."

"I brought one. It's in the back of my truck. We can make anything into a hill. It's perfect."

"I'm not sure I am up for that."

"I thought you said you were adventurous, and you wanted someone to be adventurous with?"

"I guess it's only good in theory." Addison clenched her teeth and then laughed.

Jack reassured her. "I've got you."

When he said that, everything felt right. No matter what Addison was nervous or scared about, he made it okay. He calmed her. She was a bit neurotic, and he was tranquil. He was willing to try anything, and she was a tad reserved. But both of them brought out each other's positives. And each were willing to try new things as long as they had each other's back.

Going into the last lit up igloo, it was flashing colors of white and blue. Slow instrumental Christmas music played in the background. There was a long rectangular table that had a few desserts laid out on it. Addison walked up to the items and licked her lips, scanning a mix of different shortbread cookies, a brownie, and cannoli. "I can't believe they have cannolis."

Jack smiled. "I lucked out. I guessed and ordered an assortment. I guess it was meant to be."

Addison grabbed a pistachio cannoli that was covered in a chocolate drizzle, sifted with powdered sugar. "I'll take one for the road. Let's go start our adventure." As she took a bite, the sweet cream, the crunch of the golden-brown shell, and the chopped pistachios melted in her mouth. "It's not what I usually eat on Christmas, but it's such a treat."

"What would you normally have on Christmas?" Jack asked.

"Pumpkin pie, pecan pie, and chocolate pudding pie."

Dropping his mouth open, Jack was curious. "All three?"

Addison shut her eyes and smiled. "Yep. A little bit of each one. Mom made the best pudding pie. Add a bit of whipped cream to it, and it's delicious."

"Maybe one Christmas you can make it just like she did?"

Addison smiled. "Yeah, that would be nice. I just need someone to cook for. Otherwise, I will eat the whole thing by myself."

"Do you have a lot of friends back in New York?"

"I have a few different groups of friends. I don't really talk to any of my childhood friends. Occasionally, I will reach out to a girl that I used to hang out with in high school, but she lives in California now, so it's hard to stay in contact. I have my work friends, a few work-out buddies, a couple college friends that I go to dinner with every now and then, but mostly, everyone is busy. We are all trying to survive, working our tail ends off. How about you?"

"My friends have basically stayed the same. We try to get together once a month for guys night. But everyone is married off and starting to have families."

"That has to be weird, huh? Are you envious?"

"Sometimes. Only because I know that's what I want for my life. I'm happy for them though."

Addison shook her head. "Of course."

Jack took her hand and led Addison back to their main igloo to gather his things. She enjoyed the warm touch, masculine and strong.

Addison quieted her voice and bent down to help him collect all of the things he brought. "Sorry we didn't spend much time in here. All of the igloos were so neat. I loved the different stations."

"As long as it made you smile, and you enjoyed it, that's all that matters. I had a lot of fun."

"Me too." Addison said surely.

Packing up, Jack zipped up his bag, and they walked back to the truck. The crunching of the snow against their boots made loud noises, echoing among the surrounding trees. He looked at Addison. "Tell me the last time you went sledding."

Addison tried thinking back. "I have a pretty bad memory, but probably not since middle school."

Jack laughed. "No way."

She laughed back. "Yes way."

"That's incredible. This is going to make it that much more intense."

"That statement makes me even more nervous," Addison said, gritting her teeth.

"I told you, I've got you. You don't have to worry. When I am with you, you are safe. Nothing will happen to you. I'm a doctor, remember?"

Addison rolled her eyes. "A doctor of animals. I'm not a cow. I am a human being."

Jack practically choked on his saliva, busting out laughing. "Touché."

Addison walked next to Jack until they reached the top of the hill. "You know, doctor, I did almost fall on my face yesterday."

"But did you?"

"Huh?"

"Did you? I mean, you almost did, but I caught you, right?"

Addison sighed. "Yes."

"So, like I said, don't worry. I've got you."

Addison took a deep breath and calmed her nerves. "I just feel like I'm too old for this."

"You weren't too old to do a snow angel."

Addison laughed. "Touché."

Jack placed the sled down on the ground and held it flat, allowing Addison to get on first. Then, he jumped on the back, kicking off with his feet. In a fast motion, they jumped up in the air, went flying forward, and then flung full force downward through the powdery white snow. It sprayed up into their faces, making Addison flinch. Addison dug her nails into the sled, holding on for dear life. Jack inched in closer to her, making sure she stayed firmly on the sled. He controlled it to the best of his ability by pulling the strings on the end. As they got to the bottom of the hill, Addison let out a loud gasp, thankful to be alive. She threw herself backwards, resting upon him. He looked down at her, locked eyes, and they both started laughing uncontrollably. Addison laughed so hard, she had tears rolling down her cheeks. It was exhilarating.

"Oh, my goodness, my stomach hurts, I am laughing so hard," she said.

Jack looked at her and loved her smile. He loved to see her happy. That's all he wanted. That alone made his Christmas.

Addison, being close to him and feeling drawn to him, slightly pulled herself up, meeting him face to face. His lips were quivering a millimeter away from hers. Their bodies were cold and adrenaline-fueled. She lifted her head slightly, taking him off guard, kissing the corner of his mouth and the side of his cheek. It was sensual and sweet, but not what she imagined. Mortified that he didn't meet her halfway, she moved sideways and then got off the sled.

It wasn't that he didn't want to; he did. But he wanted to make sure that he wasn't taking advantage of her. He didn't feel right having their first kiss without her knowing everything. And as much as he wanted to say it all, it was a holiday, and he didn't want to ruin the energy or mood. He wanted her to enjoy her first Christmas Eve without her mom, being happy, not sad or confused. But he could tell she felt embarrassed.

Jack got up, took the sled in his hands, smiled at her, and flirted, trying to pretend the awkward moment didn't happen. "Yep, I was right all along," he uttered.

"What's that?" she asked.

"You have the best smile."

Addison blushed and shook her head. She didn't know how to accept compliments. And she was still reeling over the moment that had just passed, feeling rejected. "Again, you are too kind."

As they walked back to the truck in silence, Jack had a smile on his face as he looked at her, taking her in amongst the sunlight. He was content and happy with the progression of their connection. But he had a big, gray cloud hanging over his head. The longer it went undiscussed, the worse he felt and the worse her reaction would be.

Addison checked her phone. "Oh, wow. We need to get back. I have a lot to do before I go to Aunt Wanda's."

"Okay. I'll take you back."

Addison leaned forward and gave him a hug. She slightly closed her eyes and held onto that feeling. She loved his natural smell, and his hair that partially smelled of fresh air and earth and partially like soap and shampoo. The back of his head, the small of his neck, the tiny scar under his left eye … she was fixated on all of it. She couldn't control her mind. It was going crazy with thoughts of him, being that close. Letting go and backing up a bit, not wanting to put herself into another awkward moment, she spun herself around with her arms out. "I needed this. Thanks, Jack."

Jack smiled. "Absolutely. Anything for you."

Addison and Jack listened to Christmas music all the way back. As he pulled in to her driveway, she was unsure about when she would see him again. Turning towards him, she placed her hand on top of his. "I don't know what to say."

Jack knew she was confused, and he didn't want her to feel anything other than happiness over their day together. "You don't have to say anything. I know. I am grateful for you too. Go have fun. I'll see you before you leave."

Again, he knew just what to say to calm her. Her shoulders immediately relaxed; her anxiety dissipated. "This was another amazing day. It's too bad I'm leaving."

"If you get time, stop by," Jack said.

Addison shook her head yes and then stepped out of the truck. "Bye."

Jack shook his head, acknowledging her departure. "Bye."

Once again, he watched her walk away and knew even more than the day before that he was head over heels. He would do absolutely anything for her. He just needed to know that she would accept him, knowing the entire truth.

Chapter 9: Choices

Addison stood at the door, marveling at the huge Christmas wreath and blow-up reindeer that surrounded the entryway. She had presents in one hand and a plate of cookies in the other. Ringing the bell, she could hear the escalation of voices as they came closer. Opening the door in the most jovial mood, Aunt Wanda leaned forward and hugged Addison. "Merry Christmas, dear. We are so glad you are here." Behind her was a group of people, cheerful and staring, awaiting an introduction. "Come on in. This is Rita, Paul, Mary, Gregg, Holland, Truvi, Nancy, and the little ones, Brie, Grace, and Izzy. A few others might be stopping by later."

Addison stood there with a big smile, pretending to be comfortable. "Hi, I am Addison." She didn't know anyone. She felt displaced. With all the focus and attention on her, it made her feel uneasy. Aunt Wanda stepped aside, giving her room and then shut the door. Taking her shoes off and setting down the gifts, she handed the plate of cookies to Aunt Wanda. "I made these specifically for you. Mom always said they were your favorite."

Aunt Wanda peeked under the cellophane and licked her lips. "Pinwheel cookies, yum. I guess my diet will start another day."

"You can't diet on Christmas," Addison said while laughing.

"The problem is, I say that every day. One of these days, I can't use that excuse any longer."

Everyone began to disperse into the living room and dining room. They were drinking out of little glass mugs with candy canes adhered to the side. Aunt Wanda looked at Addison. "This is one of my favorite holiday drinks. Peppermint Eggnog. Help yourself."

Addison grew nauseous just thinking about it. "I'm okay, thanks."

"Well, make yourself at home."

Addison slowly made her way around the room, talking to everyone. They had plenty of things to talk about, filling her in on all the town gossip. She filled a plate with appetizers: slices of cheese, prosciutto, meatballs, bacon-wrapped chestnuts, sautéed shrimp, and thyme popovers. As she sat down and filled her face, a voice from the front hallway echoed, and her body grew tense. She knew it was Jack. What was he doing here?

Trying to get the food out of her teeth, she swiped her tongue across them, grabbed a napkin and wiped her face. He came around the corner of the doorway. Immediately, he noticed her and locked eyes. He had a twinkle upon them. He smiled which made her smile. She couldn't believe he was standing there. Walking over to her, he leaned down and kissed her cheek, while also hugging her. "Merry Christmas Eve, again."

"Merry Christmas Eve. This is quite the surprise. Why didn't you tell me you were coming?"

"Your Aunt and I ran into each other in town after I left your house earlier. She asked what I was doing and mentioned that I could stop by."

"I see. Do you know any of these people?"

"Nope. Do you?"

"Nope. Like I said earlier, I feel a bit out of place."

They both laughed.

"I know you and that's all that matters," Jack said sweetly.

"You and the one-liners. You are good, Dr., You are good. You always know what to say."

"May I admit that I have ulterior motives for coming."

"I was hoping that I was the reason."

"You are leaving to go back to New York, and I realize how little time I have left with you. When you got out of my truck, I thought about the possibility of you leaving town and not seeing you again. It didn't feel right. It wasn't a proper goodbye. I've thought of a thousand different ways to kiss you. Please don't think I don't want to. I know it may have seemed that way today. I need to make sure we are on the same page. One minute I think we are, and the next, I am left confused. I didn't want to overstep today. If I let you go back to the city, and I don't tell you everything and bear my soul, then I will never be able to live with myself. I have to take that chance. Now, I'm a patient man. I'm not asking anything of you except that you listen. You can go back to New York, and we can figure it out as time moves on. I don't want to rush this. I just need you to accept my thoughts as they are and just let them resonate with you. I'm not trying to pressure you, change you, nothing ... I just have to clear my conscience."

"You can always come visit me. This doesn't have to be the last time we see each other."

Jack shook his head. He knew it was his chance to tell her how he felt and test the strength of their relationship. He couldn't wait anymore. Even though he was dead set on waiting until after the holiday, it was eating him up inside, and it didn't feel right. He couldn't be selfish. She deserved to know. He felt confident that she had spent enough time with him to get a sense of who he was and that no matter what he had to tell her, she would be more understanding and accepting. "Do you think we can go somewhere quiet for a tiny bit and talk?"

Addison grew nervous, but she needed to have clarity too. She needed it before she left. And she couldn't keep ignoring it, making him uneasy, scrambling to figure things out. It wasn't fair to him. She could tell there was a lot on his mind. "Yeah. Do you want to step outside or go in a different room?"

"Doesn't matter to me. Let's go in the back, there by the sunroom."

Addison got up and followed him. Her phone started ringing. "I'll call back."

"No, answer it. I'll wait. It's no big deal."

"Okay, I'm sorry. I don't even know who this is. It's a New York area code."

Addison clicked accept on her phone and put it up to her ear. "Hello."

"Addison, darling, this is Greyson. I thought I would give you a quick call. My assistant tried calling you, but she didn't get the details set-up. I figured I'd call myself. How is my beautiful modeling partner?"

"Oh, Greyson. Hi. I'm good, thanks. Yeah, sorry, she called me when I first got here, and I was having a moment with my mom just passing and ..."

Greyson interrupted, not wanting to hear any more. "Great, well, I just want to make sure you are still my New Year's Eve date."

Addison looked at Jack and felt a sense of guilt. Not that she was doing anything wrong, but something didn't feel right about making plans with another man. "Um ... Greyson, I have to call you back."

"Call me back? You either want to go out with me or you don't. I don't usually have to try this hard. I have a million other options, Addison. Commit, or I move on."

Addison was taken aback by his rash comment and rudeness. She rolled her eyes and felt a burn in her chest from frustration. "Maybe you should take someone else then?" She felt disposable and disrespected.

"If that's really what you want?"

Addison thought about it again for a brief second. She wanted the modeling gig, and she wasn't letting him get away with his behavior that easily. He wasn't going to take this opportunity away from her. He wasn't going to use her. She was going to use him. She could say everything that was on her mind at dinner. "Listen, I'm sorry. I have been sidetracked. Definitely, let's plan it."

"Sounds good. I've got to go. I have my hands full, so I'll be looking forward to it. A nice sleek dress, beautiful flowing hair, high heels ... I can't wait to see you."

Addison could hear a woman laughing in the background. She rolled her eyes, wondering why he was even calling her when he had someone with him. And his disgusting imagery of who he expected her to be was appalling. Who did he think he was? A manipulator and a womanizer seemed accurate.

"Yeah, okay. Bye." Addison clicked her phone off and re-collected herself.

Jack looked at her. "Who was that? You okay? You seem rattled?"

"Greyson ... the one that wants me to do the ad campaign with him. It's difficult for me to take him seriously. He's brash and chauvinistic. He makes my blood boil."

Jack side glanced at her while scrunching his forehead. "I guess you really do want to move up the ladder."

Addison was shocked by his comment, so blunt and straight-forward. It was a bit condescending, yet she knew it was true. "Well, he seemed sincere in the moment when we first discussed it. But he could use a manners and etiquette course on how to treat a woman. He can be quite awful, in your face, and pretentious. I was giving him the benefit of the doubt, because he showed a different side of himself to me the night he presented it."

"So that's what you really want?" Jack was a tad jealous and felt a bit of discomfort as frustration started bubbling up inside of him, making him tense and uneasy in his skin. He didn't want to pour his heart out if that's what she chose. He would never be enough for her.

"I mean it would help me. And don't get me wrong, I'm going to speak my mind. He's going to know that I'm not the normal girl that he is used to."

"It fits with your plan. It's everything you described to me … the dream in New York; big city, big lights, success, acknowledgment, fancy lifestyle … far away from here. You never have to come back to Edgerton."

Addison felt bad when she heard it out loud. Her dream seemed superficial. What must he think of her? She wasn't conceited or spoiled or fully focused on monetary things; she just wanted to feel that dream come to fruition after all the work she had put in. But she didn't want Jack to think she was thinking ill of Edgerton or the towns nearby. It probably seemed like she thought she was too good for such a place. Besides its charm, mostly everything she held dear here was now gone. She didn't see herself being able to build a life for herself. She didn't have her own company; she wasn't financially stable, and she didn't have a specific talent. The money she would receive from the sale of the house and store would help her out exponentially. She wouldn't have to worry about much. But she didn't want to bank her future on it, not knowing exactly what she was going to get.

The truth was … Edgerton didn't have many business opportunities, being so small. To get anywhere on a grand scale, she knew she needed a big city. She wanted a big office with the big desk, with big windows, sitting high above everyone else in a sky-rise. And she wanted one of those nameplates on her desk and on her door. At least, that's what she had envisioned when graduating with her business degree.

Being back, it was the first time she started questioning what she was doing with her life. What was her current job, really? Was it really going anywhere? What were the blood, sweat, and tears for? What was the end goal? The opportunity with Greyson proposed a new life, something she could be proud of. She finally saw the progress. Jack was a pleasant surprise into her life, but she didn't want a long-distance relationship. Every time they went down this road, about to state their feelings, she knew there was a dead end. There was no good solution. He wasn't planning on moving to the city, and she wasn't planning on moving to the country. Their connection was amazing, but if they didn't see a clear way of being together, then did it really matter?

Addison could tell that Jack seemed a bit off from her phone call. "I'm sorry for the distraction. I should have let it go to voicemail. Let's talk. What did you want to talk about?"

The mood was partially ruined by the change in energy. Jack couldn't get himself back into the right headspace. "You have a lot going on. It was nothing. Let's just enjoy the holiday."

"Really? Are you sure? You seemed pretty adamant. And I think it's important that we clear up some things."

"Yeah, I'm sure. I'm not feeling myself right now. Why don't you go join everyone in there and have a good dinner. I should be going."

"You are not going to stay?"

"No. I don't think so."

Addison was let down. "I'll stop by your dad's place before I leave," she said.

Jack shook his head. The disappointment showed in his face. He leaned towards her and gave her a hug. "Merry Christmas."

"Yeah, you too."

Walking back into the main area, Jack put his hand up to say goodbye to everyone, and he began to walk away, out the door, headed toward his vehicle.

Addison was filled with a jittery feeling and a pull in her heart. It took over her entire body. That same feeling of longing that she often felt when they parted ways. She had never felt such a way. It was very distinct, and it was only with him. Part of her wanted to run after him. They were reaching for something that seemed unattainable. They lived two vastly different lives. No matter how much they wanted it, it wasn't logical. And as much as she wanted to chase him, that kept playing in her mind and on her heart.

After Jack left, Addison was a bit off. She didn't take part in the table conversation, and she stayed quiet and to herself. Looking off, staring out the window, Addison was in her own world, unaware of the topics being discussed around her. Aunt Wanda put her hand in front of her face to get her attention. "Dear, where are you? Are you okay?"

Addison re-focused her eyes. "Huh? Oh, um, I'm sorry. I am tired."

"No problem, dear. It just seems like you have a lot on your mind. Are you missing your mom?"

"Yeah. It's difficult. But it's more than that. Everything in my life feels off. Nothing seems to be working out. I feel like it's all a mess."

"You are grieving."

"It's not just that. It's work and everything."

"Does everything include a specific gentleman that just left?"

"Maybe."

"You have a connection, you two."

Addison smirked. "We just can't get to that place. We have been trying. Something just holds us back. It's not going to work. I'm leaving. Why did I have to meet him now? Why does he have to be so wonderful?"

"These kinds of connections don't come around that often. I can attest to that. There's nothing more important than the people in your life. Who you have by your side makes your life whole. You can always find business opportunities; you just have to search for them. Yes, you might have to compromise; you might have to meet in the middle; it might take work, but if he's the one ... it's worth it, Addy. Don't let anything or anyone stand in the way. And if I might say so myself, he's a keeper. Definitely the whole package. The kind of guy every person deserves and wants."

Addison had tears filling up her eyes. She closed them, trying to regain her senses. "I don't know how he feels about me."

"Yes, you do. He's a smitten kitten in love. Everyone can tell. You know that. He knows that. I know that. The connection is real. There's a fire. I almost started sweating just watching your eye contact when he walked in. But beyond that, there's this sweetness about the two of you, the way you take each other in, the way you look for one another, the way you talk to each other."

Addison laughed. "I start sweating too. It makes me so nervous. I never let him get too close to me. I don't want get hurt again."

"What is it about Jack that makes you think he would hurt you? He's the furthest thing from that. Finish eating, go home, and think about it," Aunt Wanda said.

Addison smiled, leaned over, and gave her a hug. "That's the problem. I'm in my head too much. Like Jack says, I need to let things happen naturally instead of trying to control everything. If I looked at the positives vs. the negatives, I would stop worrying so much. If it works, it works; if it doesn't, it doesn't. But to not give it a try at all, because I'm fearful or because I don't see a clear and easy path, that's silly. Thank you. You have always given the best advice. I've never been in this situation, having so many hurdles in our way."

"Life isn't easy. Make it work. Work through the hurdles. Take it one hurdle at a time. Trust in it. If it's meant to work out, it will. No amount of distance can keep two people apart if the love is strong enough. Change your mindset and relax."

Addison heard what she was saying, but they weren't little hurdles; they were big, life decision type hurdles. Finishing up dinner and dessert, most of the guests gathered in the basement for games. Addison was ready to go home. She gave Aunt Wanda a hug and thanked her for inviting her. She walked out and felt invigorated by the cool air. She was feeling suffocated in the house. The stuffiness, the people, the heaviness of the conversation. She couldn't take any more of it. Addison spent the rest of the night thinking about Jack. Thinking up ways to make her life fit with his. She started rethinking the sale of the store and house. Maybe she could make it her own. By the time she fell asleep, she felt peace in her soul about it. She had made her decision. She would wait until tomorrow to tell him. She would risk her heart. She would compromise and make it work. He was worth the try. It would be a Christmas she would never forget. The one where she got the man of her dreams.

Chapter 10: It's Christmas

Addison woke up chipper. She had more gusto than normal. A child-like euphoria took over her body. It was Christmas day. Her favorite day of the year. The sun was shining; the house was warm; her coffee soothed her nerves, and she was ready to see Jack. The anticipation of it had her feet tingling and her arms feeling restless. Her entire body felt energized and excited.

As she walked around the family room, taking in the tree, she noticed a tiny box underneath it, way in the back. Its shiny wrapping paper left a gleam across the room as it met with the sunlight. Kneeling down, she pulled it out and shook it. She scrunched her forehead and furrowed her eyebrows. "What is this?" she asked aloud, her voice echoing through the empty room.

Sitting down, she unraveled the silver bow that was fastened around it. Gently taking off the top off the box, she looked inside. Sitting underneath white tissue paper was a pair of fourteen-carat, yellow gold, vintage-inspired, halo diamond earrings with milgrain detail. They were so stunning, her mouth dropped open. Only one person could have put them there. Jack. He must have left it under the tree when he was over last. She couldn't wait to go see him and thank him. She knew one thing for sure. They weren't friendship earrings. He was making a statement. He wanted more. It was the confirmation and confidence that she needed.

Happy that they were hopefully on the same page finally, Addison got herself ready, imagining what she would say to him. She replayed a dialogue in her head, hoping that it would all work out the way she wanted it to. Putting the final touches on her hair and make-up, she smiled in the mirror, giving herself a push of confidence. "You got this."

Fastening her coat over her chunky knit sweater, she added a light linen scarf and then headed downstairs to the garage. Taking out her phone, she searched for the address, using the number Jack had given her. Locking up and getting in her car, she put the address in her GPS, fastened her seatbelt, and set her radio to Christmas tunes as she set out to the country roads.

As the peaceful back roads soothed Addison's mind and filled her with calm, she hummed along to "All I want for Christmas." It always got her in the perfect holiday mood, full of cheer. Veering on to a windy road, coming up on a long path, Addison took in the view of a big farm. She looked at the address and then tried looking for a mailbox. She didn't see one. Her gut said that she was at the right place. Following it all the way down, she came up to an old farm house that was surrounded with barns and lots of fenced in land. A lot of it was covered in white, filled with snow and debris. Addison parked and got out. As she walked up to the door, she read a sign that was placed in the ground next to the entryway. Beardsley Farm. Happy that she was at the right property, her stomach filled with butterflies. She took a deep breath before knocking on the door. She could hear a scuffle and someone's feet shuffling along the floor trying to get to her. "I'm coming," said a male voice, older and groggy sounding. Addison grew anxious, afraid that she was disturbing him.

As the door opened slowly, Addison moved back slightly giving room. An older man looked at her, while squinting his eyes, trying to place who she was.

"Hello there," he said.

"Hi. Merry Christmas, sir. I am here to see Jack."

"Oh, well, come on in."

Addison grabbed ahold of the door. The man went and sat in his chair, moving slowly, slightly hunched over. He had the tv on, watching the news.

She followed him in, taking small steps, not knowing where to go. "Is he home?"

"Oh, he's out. He will be back soon. He is tending to an animal. You can sit down and wait for him."

"Oh, um, okay." Addison made her way to the couch next to him. She sat down and crossed her legs, putting her hands together.

He looked at her. "Can I make you something?"

"No, no. I am good."

"Are you a friend of Jack's?" he asked.

"I'm Addison. Jack and I have become friends since I have been back here in Edgerton."

"That's nice. Great to meet you, Addison. I'm Jack's dad. James."

"He's told me so much about you."

"He has, huh? I hope it's good stuff. He hasn't left me alone lately."

"He just wants to be with you and take care of you, since we have had so much snow."

James looked at Addison and smiled. He looked at her more intently than he had before, as if he was trying to make sense of something. It made her feel a bit uncomfortable.

"You have a great smile. It reminds me of someone," he said.

"Thank you." Addison looked away, hoping Jack would walk through the door.

James started to get up but had a hard time mustering the strength. "I'm getting too old. I sit in this chair too long."

"Are you trying to go somewhere? Can I help you?" Addison asked. She stood up and put out her hand for him to hold on to.

"I left my slippers in the bedroom. I was going to get them."

"Don't get up. I will get them. Are you comfortable with that?"

"That would be great, thanks. They are next to the bed." He pointed to his bedroom.

Addison walked to the bedroom door and pushed it open. As she looked around, she searched for the slippers on the floor. Going to the other side of the bed and leaning over to grab them, she noticed something out of the corner of her eye. She felt bad, looking at his personal things, but something drew her in that she couldn't take her sights off of. A stack of drawings behind the door. Going closer, she flipped through them, one by one. Seeing the one she gave Jack, she smiled. But there were multiple others behind it. Ones she had never seen before and then the ones that were bought from the open house. She couldn't breathe. She was in shock. Her chest hurt. She tried taking small breaths to control herself. Confusion took over, as she tried to piece it together. She was squinting, her mind was cloudy, and her heart was breaking. She had a bad feeling.

Jack's footsteps could be heard walking through the house. He walked into the bedroom. "Addison ..."

Addison moved around the door to see him. "What? ... why?" She couldn't get the right words out.

"I can explain."

"Go for it," she said.

"The paintings are my dads'. I had never seen the ones in your shop before. They looked similar to his other ones, but I wasn't sure. It was a weird feeling seeing such a portrait. He has always drawn much more subdued things, not so 'in your face'. I knew it was his when I saw the initials, but I wanted to ask him about it before I said anything."

"Okay. That's pretty simple, why didn't you just tell me that? I would have given them to you. How did you get the rest of them? I sold them to a lady."

"It was a business associate of mine. They called and made the deal with you."

"Why the secrecy? I'm confused."

"There's more."

"Go on then …" Addison was starting to get frustrated and hot.

"The woman in the painting is your mom."

"What? No." Addison couldn't believe what he was saying.

"Yes. My dad and your mom."

Addison's eyes widened, and she gulped. Her stomach dropped. She put her hand over her mouth, thinking it over. *How could this be?* She was befuddled. She furrowed her eyebrows and then looked at Jack as if he was crazy. "You can't be serious? No. She wasn't with anyone; she would have told me."

"Actually, they have been together for quite a while. Years, actually. They were in love."

Addison had tears billowing up in her eyes. How could she be the last one to know? How could no one tell her? She felt betrayed and embarrassed. "Of all people … You hid this from me. You knew. You broke my trust. You let me talk and talk, and all the while, you knew this big secret. I told you about my dad. How could you? I asked you if they knew each other, multiple times, and you said you didn't know. I had you in my home. I showed you pictures of her."

194

"I didn't know all the details. I was trying to piece it together. My dad wasn't open about it either. He kept talking about Mona's, and I figured it was a long shot to go in there and see what it was all about. I wanted to see what had him so distracted. I didn't realize that he was grieving her death. When I brought the painting home, we had a long talk because he was overcome with emotion and the memory attached to it. He admitted to me that they had a serious relationship. I was shocked. Neither one of them wanted to tell us because they wanted their love to be private, not affecting our lives. They wanted us to remember our parents, and they didn't know how we would take it, them being in love again. They were afraid that we would oppose them moving on."

"I would never."

"I wouldn't either, but I do have to admit, seeing that portrait, full of passion, so in love, I'm not sure I even saw him that way with my own mom. I felt a little uncomfortable. It was hard to come to terms with. I can't say I liked it at first. Then I thought about how special it is to find two strong loves in your life, especially a love later in life. And you helped me see how wonderful your mom was and why my dad loved her so much."

"I'm just so upset that she didn't feel she could tell me. That I made her feel so disconnected and unimportant to me that she had a whole other life that I didn't know about."

"Just the way you talked about your dad to me, you probably talked about him to her, and she didn't know how. She didn't want to ruin that for you. And like you said, you were busy in New York."

"More than anything, I wanted her to be happy. It would have given me such a sense of peace knowing someone was taking care of her."

"I know. Me too."

"I'm still really shocked and disappointed about your role in all of this. It isn't fair. All that time you spent with me, it was to figure out a storyline?"

"No, not at all. I mean, it started out that way, to learn more about her, to get to know you, but it was real. The way I feel about you is real. I didn't expect that."

"And how do you feel about me? I think I can tell, by little things you say, but you never make a move. I question it, back and forth, all of the time. Besides the beautiful earrings you left for me. I think that makes a statement. Thank you for those, by the way. But I'm thinking, now, it might be best if you keep them."

"I have tried so many times to say how I feel and to tell you about this. And I didn't want to make a move until you knew everything. I respect you too much. I won't take that moment away from you, just to fill my selfish needs of wanting to be close to you. I want you to want me, but I need to know that you still feel that way, after knowing all of this. I want to be with you, but I don't want it clouded by anything. And, I don't want the earrings back. I want you to have them."

Addison gulped, trying to control her emotions. "One of the things I loved the most about you was your honesty. But you are not honest. You are not who I thought you were."

"That's not fair. I never lied. I just never said anything."

"To me, that's the same thing."

"Like I said, I was going to. A few times, actually. But something always stopped me."

Moving past Jack, Addison went back into the living room and handed James his slippers. "Here you go." She gave him a soft smile and looked him over. She wanted to hug him and talk to him, asking him detail after detail. But she didn't want to be disrespectful.

"Thank you, dear," he said.

She tried pushing her feelings down, so she wouldn't cry in front of him. Looking at his face, she couldn't think of anything else but that fact that her mom loved him. He was a part of her. And yet, Addison didn't know him at all. He was a complete stranger. How could that be? It was surreal. She knelt down on the floor and looked up at him. "Let me put them on your feet for you."

He smiled. "I'm getting too old, huh?"

Addison smiled. "With age comes wisdom. You may not be able to move like you used to, but I bet you are smarter than all of us. You have this life thing figured out. I have to get going, but I would love to speak to you sometime. Maybe I can come back?"

He shook his head yes. Looking at her, he looked into her eyes with recognition. "I figured out who your smile reminds me of. My dear Mona."

Addison started to cry. "I'm sorry. Don't mind me. I am a mess today. Being Christmas and all."

Jack stood behind his dad's chair. "Dad, this is Mona's daughter."

James leaned forward, and his jaw started trembling. His eyes were watery. He tried grabbing her hand.

Addison looked up at Jack. "I need to go." She touched James' hand slightly for a moment and then gently pulled her hand away, got up, turned around, and walked out. She walked fast enough that Jack couldn't stop her. She heard his voice calling out to come back, but she blocked him out.

Getting in her car, she sped down the road. Her tires spun in the snow and slid to the side. She put the car in park and rested her head on the steering wheel to compose herself. She was confused and flustered. Everything rushed through her head. She had so many feelings. Jack, most of all, being the biggest disappointment. Her plans to tell him that she loved him fell away. She felt silly for contemplating leaving New York for him, keeping the antique store, and staying in Edgerton to make it work. That was no longer an option. It wasn't real. None of it.

After a few minutes, Addison pulled herself together and headed back home. She wanted to be alone. It was a rather peaceful drive. Everything was glistening in the sun. Before she knew it, she turned into her driveway, turned off the car, and released the tension built up in her body. She had one thing on her mind. She was going to search through everything. She wanted to find some kind of evidence that proved their relationship.

Addison was on auto pilot as she went through the motions and walked to the attic. She felt a bit numb. Having already sifted through many boxes in the basement and closets, she thought the attic might have something. She pulled down the ladder from the ceiling and climbed the stairs. Pulling the string on the light, making it brighter, she looked around. There was a stack of old insulation, lumber, tools, and fishing poles. But she couldn't see anything of interest. She started walking around, moving things little by little. Pulling off a blue blanket, she found an old chest. Opening it, it was filled with art supplies. She took things out, trying to get to the bottom. Under all of it, was a stack of chalk illustrations. They were striking. She pulled them out and looked at them, one by one. A few of them were random, one being of a cat and a few others being different flowers and plants. The rest were portraits of people. Addison didn't know who they were, except for the last couple. They were of her mom, beautiful as ever. She looked so happy. He captured her in a way that made her shine. But still, there was no proof or evidence of their long, loving relationship. Addison huffed, wanting clarity and resolution. She didn't want to go back to the city without it.

Going back downstairs, she went into her room and pulled out the note her mom had left her. She re-read the sentence "don't be upset with me." It made sense now. Speaking out loud, to the empty room, Addison spoke to her mom's spirit. "Mom, I am not mad at you. I am mad at myself. I am glad you had someone. I wish for the same thing. Please guide me to finding happiness. I have been a wreck for too long. I miss you, and I love you. I will check in on him, I promise."

As she set the note on the side table, a thought came to her. *Check Mom's bedroom.* Rushing into her mom's room, she started pulling drawers open. Socks, underwear, shirts, pants. Nothing. She went by her vanity. Jewelry, perfume, hair pins, make-up. Nothing. She looked under the bed. Nothing. She went into the bathroom and looked around. Opening the cabinets, she saw toiletries but nothing else. Going into her closet, she started looking around, moving clothes to the side that hung from different racks. It wasn't until she got on the floor and looked up, trying to see if anything was hidden that she noticed on the very bottom, a long, rectangular, clear organizing bin. Pulling it out, the cover had a piece of tape on it. It was marked "my love." Just reading those words irked Addison in the slightest. Thinking of it being another man other than her dad felt strange. Yet, this was what she wanted. She wanted to see it with her own eyes.

The bin was filled with mementos of their life together. Everything was labeled with dates. Love notes, cards, menus from the restaurants they had dates in, dried roses, and pictures. Many, many pictures. Addison could see their love. It was laid out before her. Clear as day, simple and true. Their similarities, their smiles, their connection. The words they said to one another, their loyalty and commitment so strong. They were undoubtedly in love, passionately and fiercely. It brought a smile to her face, and tears ran down her cheek.

A foot stepped into the room, making the floor creak. She turned her head to see who it was. "Addison?"

Addison looked at Jack and bit her lip. "Well, I found the proof."

He walked forward, knelt down on the floor, and hugged her. "I never meant to hurt you. No one did. I came to say I'm sorry. I was in the wrong. You are right. I held information from you, and that wasn't fair. I was scared. I didn't want anything ruining what we were building. I couldn't let our disagreement at my dad's house be the last time I saw you."

"Please tell your dad I'm sorry. I didn't mean to run out of there like that. That was rude of me. My mom would be disappointed in me. Maybe she already was and that's why she never told me or introduced us."

"No. You know that's not true."

"Well, it just doesn't make sense. I would never not tell her if I had a long love affair with someone. Why didn't she tell me?"

"I don't know. I'm not her. My dad didn't tell me either. Please know that if I could, I would do things a lot differently. You know I'm not a deceitful person."

"I want to let it go, I do. But I keep going back to the fact that you lied. The first day we met, you knew. You were looking at that stuff because you knew. I'm such a fool. I could feel something, but I didn't know what it was. What else could you hide from me? That's the real question."

"Honestly, I didn't know that my dad was still doing art. When I saw that one in the window, I thought it might be his, but I wasn't sure. It took me back."

"I need to know … exactly when did you find out for sure?"

"My dad told me bits and pieces when I brought it home. I had never seen anyone with him besides my mom. For me, it was difficult at first. I didn't want to hear about it. Then, I started thinking about who she was, how they met, what made her so special. I wanted to know more about her. She had his heart, I could tell. I wanted to connect with him in some way. I wanted to help him. He seemed so distraught."

"So, you have known almost the whole time. Basically, since the night we met."

"I had a feeling, yes. I wasn't one hundred percent sure. I didn't want to say anything not knowing enough detail."

"Other people must have known about this too. Which makes it even worse. All the little comments. They have been replaying in my head. Aunt Wanda knew, and she said nothing. No wonder she liked seeing us together."

"Can you blame them? Is it so wrong to want happiness for two people?"

"This isn't going to work. I'm leaving tonight. This is all too much. It's too heavy on my heart. Love isn't supposed to be this hard. It's supposed to be easy."

Jack stopped her. "Love?"

"You know what I mean. Something romantic."

"Explain. Too much what? Cause from where I stand, it's exactly what we both need. It's what I want. And I think deep down, if you are honest with yourself, it's what you want. Isn't that why you stopped at my dad's house today? Or is that me being hopeful? This feels right. This feels like how it's supposed to be. Did you ever think that maybe we were meant to meet the way we did? Love isn't always easy. You have to fight for it. It takes a lot of effort sometimes. But I'm willing to do that."

Jack leaned forward while sitting on his knees next to her, pulling her closer to him. He put his hands on hers and brought them up to his mouth, kissing the tops. Then he leaned forward and kissed the side of her forehead by her temple. He put both of his hands on the sides of her face and kissed her cheek. He kissed her ear. Addison's throat went dry, and goosebumps formed on her arms. He tried going for her lips, but she pulled away just a little, giving him a hint that she was uncomfortable. She was upset, and even though it felt so good to be near him, she couldn't ignore the feeling of betrayal.

Addison closed her eyes for a second and sucked in her lips. She tried controlling herself. Re-opening her eyes and looking at him, she took a deep breath. "I don't know what to believe anymore, because the whole thing feels tainted now. I don't know what is real. I woke up today with a clear mind and an open heart. I wanted to profess my feelings to you, and I wanted to see where we could go from here. I was willing to compromise. Actually, I was ready to leave it all. Everything. I was planning on calling Martha today. I actually thought about taking the store and house off the market. I was going to do that for you. For us. It would have been a drastic change, but I was ready to try. I thought it would be the Christmas of my dreams, where I got my dream guy, and everything fell into place. But, it just doesn't feel right anymore."

"How can you just turn your feelings off?"

Addison knew what he was getting at. He wanted to be with her, a full commitment moving forward, and he wanted their connection to be enough. Before all of this, she wanted to be with him too. She stayed quiet, not answering.

Putting his hand on her leg, he looked at her lovingly. "Do you really have to go? Can you stay? Can you give this more time? A few more days is all I'm asking."

"I have to get back to work." Addison knew she could stay if she wanted to. Reality was, she didn't want to. She was ready to go back to the city. She needed to get out of Edgerton. She was caught up in a web of deceit, and it didn't feel good with her soul.

"Are you sure that you can't stay for the new year? I can't convince you to cancel your date?" He was begging and pleading, looking at her with serious intent and hopefulness.

"I told you, it's a business meeting."

Jack shook his head, disappointed. He was trying to be understanding. His throat went dry thinking of her leaving and never seeing her again. He was losing her. "So, you won't have anything to come back for then. I guess this is it. This is goodbye."

Addison grew a bit cold towards him. "Yeah. I guess it is. I do want to stay in contact with your dad in some way. I think it's what my mom would have wanted. I want to make sure he is doing well."

"Sure. He would love that."

"I have to admit, as much as I dreaded this trip, coming back and surrounding myself with my mother's things, it was nice. It was peaceful, and I enjoyed it. I tied up all the loose ends and learned things about her that I never anticipated. I even learned a little bit about antiques. Who would have thought? She would have loved that. I'm going to call this the Christmas of antiques. No, even better, an antique Christmas. I will never forget it." Addison had a sly smile on her face. "It was nice to have someone to hang with. Thank you."

"Yeah. A good hang out buddy. That's always something to be remembered by." Jack laughed through his sarcasm.

"That's not what I meant, and you know it. I wish things could have turned out differently."

"I know. I'm just making light of the situation. I'll miss you."

"I'll miss you too. If you ever come to New York, please call me."

"Same with you. Come to Waterford whenever you want. Or Edgerton. My dad's door is always open, as well as mine."

Jack fought his internal desires. He loved her. He didn't want to hold her back, making her stay in a place that she didn't want to be. He cared too much for her. She deserved to find her happiness and fulfill her dreams without looking at him and feeling disgust and anger.

They headed downstairs and walked towards the front door. Addison leaned forward and hugged him. Closing her eyes while embracing, Addison let his energy consume her for the last time. She reveled in his smell, that of sandalwood and soap. "Bye," she whispered. Pulling away, she backed up and separated her body from his.

"Best of luck," he said. He walked out and pulled the door shut behind him.

"See you around, Jack," Addison said aloud to the quiet room before her.

She discreetly watched from the corner of the window as he pulled away. The feeling she had inside of her was tugging at her heart. She felt uneasy and unsettled. She couldn't tell if it was saying goodbye, overall, knowing she was leaving her childhood house, leaving Edgerton and everything that connected her to her parents, or leaving Jack. She just knew in order to get over the feeling, the best thing to do was go back to New York.

Addison went room by room, making sure things were tidy and stripped down. She put some personal things in boxes and then went upstairs to pack her belongings. Once she felt everything was in order, she went to her car, shoving it all in and slamming the trunk to make sure it stayed down. Knowing it might be the last time she stepped foot on the property, Addison went up on the porch and took it in. The windows, the shutters, the door, the porch, the trees, everything. It was like the finale of a decade-long sitcom. It had to come to an end, and it couldn't be stopped. Placing the key in a lock box that Martha had set up, Addison said a little prayer. Knowing Martha was going to be at the house staging it and showing it, she could only hope a deal would work out soon. Addison didn't want to give the house away. She knew it was worth a pretty penny, but she wanted to be rid of the burden. She was ready for a fresh start.

Chapter 11: A Fresh Start

Christmastime in New York was a sight to behold. The holiday decorations, the array of lights, and ornate window displays were bewitching. Holiday markets, ice skating, nativity scenes, it was alluring. The city was full of spirit. Tourists from all over the world visited New York to see its larger-than-life Christmas tree, twinkling landscape, and to feel its mystical appeal. Addison felt lucky to call it home. As she walked out of her building and down the street, she admired the giant, red Christmas ornaments at the end of her block, as she passed them, heading to the nearest coffee shop. Being back, it was the first time she felt the drastic difference between city life and suburbia. As much as she loved New York, and she missed its diverse, magnetic, eclectic, intoxicating aura, a part of her felt empty. Maybe she was missing the quaint, friendly, and cheery demeanor of Edgerton? Or, its peaceful and quiet atmosphere? For the first time ever, she found herself resenting the commotion, loudness, and rush of people. Who was she? She didn't recognize these thoughts. Maybe it was her lingering grief, forming a dark cloud over her mood, feeling like a depression? Or, maybe it was the way she left Edgerton, having a disagreement with Jack? Regardless, it was a new normal, and she had to get used to it.

Going into the coffee shop, she ordered her usual caramel macchiato and waited. She watched as a family dined together at a table in the corner, drinking hot chocolate and sharing pie. They were smiling and laughing, doting on each other. Addison zoned in on the little girl, watching her innocence. The way she looked at her mom and dad, it was a tender moment filled with love and happiness. What she wouldn't do to have a moment like that once more.

Smiling at the sweetness, she found herself in a stare. A voice startled her. "Addison."

Turning around, she made eye contact with a young teenage boy that was standing by the counter, looking at her, holding her coffee. Snapping her out of her trance, she grabbed her drink politely and grinned. "Thank you. Merry Christmas."

As she walked out and headed back to her apartment, she felt that loneliness creep up again. Nothing felt the same. And to make it worse, she couldn't believe that she was alone on Christmas. No one to have dinner with. She knew she could call a friend or two, but they had their own families to attend to, and she didn't want to disrupt their togetherness.

Getting back, Addison sat in her apartment looking out the window and sitting next to the phone. The television played old black and white movies, but she wasn't in the mood. Bored, she contemplated calling Jack many times. Instead, she called her voicemail and listened to the last message that her mom left her. She smiled, and her eyes filled with tears hearing her mom's kind, soft-spoken voice fill the room. "Hi, Addy. It's Mom. I found the most interesting thing today at the flea market. Call me back. I've been thinking of you. Hope you are doing good. I miss you, sweetheart. Love you always." It made her happy and sad at the same time, but it soothed her as it played on repeat. Before she knew it, her eyes drifted off to sleep, her body feeling comforted, pretending her mom was with her.

As the days went by, time passed slowly, and Addison went back to her normal schedule. Work, home, work, home. Everything was becoming monotonous. It was energy sucking. She was looking forward to New Year's Eve, so she could solidify the partnership with Greyson and change the routine.

It was the day before their dinner. Addison went into the office to do double the work load, so she didn't have to come in on New Year's Eve and cover anyone's shift. After sorting through files, getting coffees for the office staff, entering data in the computer, making spreadsheets, printing off account information, and making calls for collections, Addison was done. She was exhausted. Every ounce of her wanted to turn in her resignation letter and never come back. As her head thumped and her shoulders grew tense, making her neck kink up, a thought popped in her head. *Had she outgrown Doxens? Why was she still there, allowing them to use her? Why did she put up with so much?* She had never been so ready to leave for the day. Her feet hurt, and she was desperately seeking peace and quiet. Grabbing her stuff, she clocked out, left the building, and started walking home. As she walked home, she thought about her dinner with Greyson. For a moment, she grew scared, thinking of Jack's warnings. But then, the anticipation of having a new job title made her excited. She was ready for a new direction. It was time. Time for a change. Time to make herself happy.

She didn't want to waste any more of her youth working a tireless and thankless job with no change in sight. She couldn't even think of stepping foot in Doxens again doing the same type of grunt work. It was going to change, or she was ready to move on. That was her New Year's resolution to herself.

As she looked up, it was a dreary day with grayish skies. She felt the way the city looked, gloomy and overcast. Staying to herself and walking briskly to surpass the crowd, a taxi cab sped by her, honking, making her jump. Addison moved further away from the curb and walked around a construction site, full of jack hammering and drilling, only to get smogged by a plume of steam rising from the ground near a manhole cover. She ducked and held her breath. As she continued walking, she exhaled and then took a large whiff of sewer smell. "Ugh," she groaned. Wincing and plugging her nose, she grew disgusted. Normally, it didn't bother her. Today, it was making her nauseated. She couldn't place why everything felt so negative. Veering over to her street, she came upon her building's entrance. Walking up the steps and going inside, she went up one flight of stairs. Taking out her keys, she unlocked the door and went inside. She rested against the hard oak door after she shut it. She took a deep breath and started to feel choked up. Everything was overwhelming her. Anxiety took over, and she felt like she was suffocating. Undoing her scarf, taking off her jacket, and placing everything on a side chair, she went straight into her bathroom and started the water to fill the tub. As it started to fill up, she got in. Letting the hot water hit her skin, she closed her eyes and zoned out.

It was the best few minutes of her day, and she felt completely relaxed. Her phone began ringing, sending her back into stress-mode. Trying to sit up, she grabbed a towel from the floor, and picked up her phone from the sink counter. Somewhere deep down inside, she hoped it might be Jack. She had missed their conversations immensely.

"Hello," she answered, frazzled and hopeful.

"Addison, it's Greyson. How are you?"

Addison, a little disappointed after realizing it wasn't Jack, tried getting herself in a chipper mood. "Oh, Greyson. It's so nice to hear from you. I am really looking forward to our dinner tomorrow. I'm hoping everything is on schedule as planned?"

"Absolutely. I can't wait to see you. I have big plans for us."

Addison widened her eyes and silently mouthed words in the mirror, as she looked at herself. "I bet you do."

"Addison, are you still there?"

"Yeah, sorry. Um … I can't wait to see what you have planned. Where should we meet?"

"There's a big bash at Hotel Posh. We can do dinner and dancing and figure it out from there. I booked us a room, just in case we didn't want to deal with transportation fiascos. Or in case you needed to freshen up. I want you to feel comfortable."

Addison was surprised he was being thoughtful, even if his intentions weren't as pure as she'd like them to be. "That's very kind of you. Thank you. I will meet you there. What time is good?"

"I'll send a limo. It will be there at 4:00."

"I appreciate it. See you then."

"It's been too long. Can't wait to see your pretty face. I must be the luckiest guy in New York. Until tomorrow."

"Yep. Until tomorrow." Addison hung up and smiled.

Part of Greyson's charm warmed her up. He had a softness in his voice that she found appealing. It felt good to be wanted, to be complimented, to be sought after. While most of the time, his come-ons were cheesy and somewhat repulsive, it was a nice change and a good distraction. Maybe she hadn't seen all of his sides yet? Maybe there was more depth to him, and the arrogance was just for show? She could only hope. And she could use some of his upbeat energy.

Hopping back into the bath, she submerged herself in the hot, soapy water and fell back into her trance.

It was New Year's Eve, a day of celebration. A day of reflecting and renewal. As Addison woke up, she felt exactly that … renewed. She didn't have the same doom and gloom hanging over her as the night before. There was an excitement, knowing she had plans, knowing this year was ending, and the next was beginning. Nerves and anticipation made her antsy and nostalgic. She was going to an elite party, filled with all the high and mighties of Manhattan. Every wealthy business person and top-name socialite would be attending. It was like being a part of the rich and famous. Her little girl dreams were coming true. She went to the closet and pulled out her classiest dress. A sleek, black number that fit her curves just right. It was a stretch-woven fabric with thick straps that supported a sweetheart neckline, a princess seamed bodice, and a straight cut midi skirt with a sultry side slit. She hung it on a clothing rack by itself, making sure it didn't wrinkle. Searching through her shoes in her closet, she found the perfect set of heels. A pair of black, suede 4" stilettos with a single toe band and an ankle strap anchored by a slender heel cup. Looking at her ensemble, she needed to finish it off with something shiny. She pulled out a layered necklace of small, circular rhinestone charms on two gold chains and looked over her earrings. She gravitated towards a pair of tear-drop rhinestone earrings but then immediately shifted to the one thing that kept grabbing her attention. The earrings that Jack gave her were in a little black box, resting in the corner on her dresser. She had been trying to ignore them, forgetting about everything, but something within her pushed her to pick them up. Snapping it open, the beauty and sparkle immediately hit her eyes and impressed her, making her melt a little bit. While they symbolized

215

something that was no longer available to her, something about them made her feel like home. Just looking at them made her feel comforted. Swapping them out and putting the other earrings back, she stepped back and looked everything over. "Simple, classy, elegant, pretty," she said out loud. Happy with her decisions, she headed to the kitchen to give herself some pep.

As she brewed a pot of coffee and heated up a bowl of oatmeal, she sat at the counter and read the paper. She couldn't stop envisioning herself as one of the models in the ads she was looking at. She would be the face of Doxens. Her face would be everywhere. People would be looking at her as they read their magazine or paper in the morning drinking their coffee. She would be who they saw when they turned on their tv, and a commercial popped on the screen. She would become a well-known name. It seemed odd when she thought of it that way.

As Addison finished up and cleared the dishes, she looked at her phone. She had a text from Martha. Opening it up, her mouth dropped.

Martha: Addison, Great news. We have a buyer. It took a little longer than I thought, but we were dealing with multiple offers. I wanted to make sure you got the highest one. They are paying full asking price on the store. I will send over the paperwork. Congratulations.

Addison was happy, but it was bittersweet. Reading that made her instantly shift her thinking back to Edgerton, her mom, and Jack. The things that made her feel so sad. And even though it felt good having a buyer, a small twinge of regret plagued her, knowing it wasn't hers anymore. For a slight moment, she wondered if she made a mistake; If it was a missed opportunity. She texted Martha back.

Addison: Thank you, Martha. Any news on the house?

Martha: I am working on it. There's a lot of interest. I wouldn't be surprised if we got an offer in the next week. Happy New Year.

Addison: Happy New Year.

Addison set her phone down on the counter. She was curious and couldn't help but wonder. What was Jack doing? How was he? Was he sad too? The thought of him kissing someone at the stroke of midnight made her feel ill. She tried getting the vision out of her head. She didn't want all of that on her mind going into her meeting with Greyson. Setting down a workout mat, she began doing her stretches and exercises, loosening her body. It took twenty minutes to realize that nothing would get it out of her head. His piercing kind eyes, his masculine chin, his adorable smile, his calming nature, it flashed over and over again in her mind. It was an incessant thought that she was obsessing over, and it didn't feel good. Why was she thinking of him so much?

Trying to stay distracted, she went into full adrenaline mode. Putting on her music, she ran in place, she did jumping jacks, lifted weights, used her exercise bands, and did stair steps. As she sweat it out, she began to feel better. But it didn't curb it all together.

For the next while, to waste time and put her sights elsewhere, Addison watched old movies, getting into the New Year's Eve mood. She painted her nails, she lotioned up her legs, and she did a luminizing charcoal mask on her face, so she'd look young and dewy. She was feeling very melancholy and knew she needed a jolt of vim and vigor. Checking the clock, and realizing it was inching closer to four o'clock, she jumped in the shower, letting the water hit her face, awakening her senses. Then, she began to prepare, taking out her make-up and curling iron. As she began to get ready, she looked in the mirror. While something in her yearned for this dinner and opportunity, something in her gut made her feel like she shouldn't go. Was is it anxiety? Was it fear? Were Jack's concerns playing a toll? Or were her instincts warning her? She pushed her negative feelings down and kept moving, going with the motions.

After drying her hair, she kept it long and wavy. Using a large barrel curling iron, she made loose, flowing curls throughout. Applying her make-up with a glamorous look in mind, she did a gold smoky eye, full false lashes, a berry colored lipstick, and a shimmering soft pink on her cheeks, highlighted with a misty glow upon her cheekbones. Going into her room, she slipped on her dress, shoes, and jewelry, adding a bit of shimmer to her skin with a finishing mist. Smelling like jasmine, gardenia, and honeysuckle, she put her perfume back on her night stand, went to the closet to grab a black wristlet, and headed to the front hallway to put on a white, formal, long-sleeve, stand collar, black button trench coat. Walking out in a hurry, making sure she didn't miss the limo, she locked the bottom door knob and shut it behind her.

Addison walked out of her building and liked what she saw. Standing there, dapper and gentlemanly, was a chauffeur, awaiting her presence, with the door open. He was an older gentleman with gray hair, a mustache, and a sweet smile.

As she got closer to him, she gave him a sweet smile right back. "Hello, Sir."

He tipped his hat at her. "Hello, Ma'am. I assume you are Ms. Monroe?"

"Yes, I am."

"Welcome. I am Stan. I will be your driver. I am directed to take you to Mr. Herrington at Hotel Posh. He is waiting for you."

"That is correct. Thank you."

Addison ducked her head and slid her way in, holding her dress down, so she was lady-like. Stan shut her door and went around to the driver's seat.

Stan looked back at her. "You look beautiful by the way."

"Oh, thank you." Addison blushed. "I like your suit."

Stan smiled. "That's sweet of you."

"Do you have plans tonight, Stan?"

"I'm working."

"I'm sorry. But I bet you get a lot of business on New Year's Eve. You will probably be working till the wee hours of the morning."

"Don't be sorry. This is what I do. I get to meet nice people like you."

Stan seemed like a gentle soul. He reminded her of a grandfather figure, soft-spoken, warm-hearted, and nurturing. "Where are you from, Stan?"

"I'm originally from Iowa. My family is back there."

"I bet you miss them. That's far away."

"I sure do. I think about going back all the time. I miss it there. I'd like to retire in the countryside."

Addison immediately thought of Edgerton. "There is something pretty special about the countryside, isn't there?" She never thought she would say that. But hearing it come out of her mouth, she realized she had changed. Her visit had indelibly changed her. And if she was honest, she didn't know how to go on without it now. She missed it.

"It's serene. I miss having land. I used to live on lots and lots of land," Stan said.

"That sounds special. I hope you get to go back there soon," Addison said.

Stan pulled up curbside. "Well, Ma'am, we are here. I will come around and open the door for you."

Addison stopped him. "Please don't. I'm good. I can let myself out. Thank you for driving me. It has been a pleasure meeting you. Enjoy your night. Happy New Year."

Surprised at her answer, Stan tilted his head at her. "You, too."

As Addison headed inside, she was in awe. The front of the hotel and the entrance to the lobby were decorated with thousands of lights. She felt like a movie star.

A man greeted her in the lobby. "Hello, how can I help you? Are you joining the New Year's festivities?"

"Yes, I am. I am meeting someone here."

"Mr. Herrington, by chance?"

Addison shook her head shyly. "Mm-hm ... yep."

"Great. Right this way."

Addison thought it over. Was this Greyson's normal dating ritual? Did he come here so often with women that the staff knew his routine? Or was this set-up just for her? She wasn't sure, but she was suspicious.

Standing by the bar, as they walked down a long walkway, Greyson waited for her. Addison forgot how handsome he was. He was striking at first glance. He was dressed in a black notch lapel tux with a white undershirt, black tie, and folded white pocket square. He looked sharp. Seeing Addison, his eyes lit up. He walked closer to her. "Well, hello, beautiful."

Addison smiled but stayed coy. "Hello."

"You look more amazing than I remembered. That dress, those earrings. Wow."

Addison smiled and touched her earrings, thinking of Jack.

"Why don't you follow me. I have a place for us at the table."

Addison was confused. A place for us? What did he mean by that? She thought it was just the two of them for dinner. Following him into a large, open room, he brought her to a table filled with people. Immediately, she felt extremely uncomfortable. No warm welcomes but a lot of eyes darting her direction to give her a judgmental once over. Men winking at her and giving her the eye. Women turning up their noses at her. It only took Greyson a matter of minutes to set his sights on something else. He was quickly in the arms of two buxom blondes, dancing and showing off. She stood there looking around, wondering why she was there. Were they even going to discuss the campaign, or was it all a lie … a bluff … a fallacy? She was starting to wonder if he used his power and social standing just to lure her there. Looking at him, feeling grossed out by his cocky, handsy, immature, and in your face macho persona, she wanted to leave. Turning around, she started to walk away. Greyson called out for her, but she kept walking. She rolled her eyes feeling completely humiliated. He didn't really want her there. He was too amused with the young twenty-year-old's vying for his attention.

Catching up to her, Greyson walked in front of her. "Addison, hey, where are you going? You just got here. Stop. C'mon. Have some fun. Loosen up a bit. Let me get you something. Anything. You name it."

"It seems like you are having fun. I don't want to interrupt."

"You can be part of the fun. That's why I invited you."

"I thought we were having dinner to talk about the campaign. Was that a lie?"

"No, we can. It's just not a formal thing. We can talk about it right now. What do you want to discuss? You want to do the campaign, great. I'll tell Mr. Lambert. Done. It's as easy as that, see? You worry for nothing. Now, let loose and enjoy the night." Greyson creepily moved closer to her body.

Addison backed away, repulsed by his advances and blatant disregard for her feelings. "You haven't even told him yet?"

"No, but I will. He will let me do whatever I want. Come sit. I will have the waiter get you something to drink."

Addison hemmed and hawed. She finally obliged to be polite and walked back to an empty chair, sitting down. Greyson sat down beside her. He kept trying to put his arm around her, but she maneuvered out of it. As handsome as he was, his personality just didn't follow suit. Listening to him brag, talk disrespectfully, and continue to be misogynistic, she couldn't stomach him. He made her skin crawl when he spoke. And he wasn't the only one. Everyone at the table seemed to have the same views and thoughts. Addison wanted to blurt out unkind things and put them in their place, but she knew it wouldn't do any good. As she grew quieter, distancing herself from him, Greyson got up to say hi to someone across the room. He was over-the-top, getting louder and louder by the minute. His voice carried across the room. If he wasn't the center of attention, he made a spectacle, so he couldn't be ignored. And Addison was done.

Listening to the conversations next to her, so superficial and drama-filled, she began to contemplate her life. Was this what she wanted? Was this the dream she had for herself? With these kinds of people? With a man like Greyson? She didn't want to associate with someone that had no regard for other people. He was a showboat, someone that could turn things on and off, depending on who he was around. Nothing about him was real. Why was she wasting her time? This could be her life if she went down this path. Maybe she wasn't giving them a chance, but she knew it in her heart, she wasn't in the right place. It wasn't for her. Everything she imagined: the fame, stature, connections, and money. It wasn't what she had imagined. And it meant nothing. It wasn't going to make her happy. For the first time since being back in New York, her mind was clear. She knew what she wanted. She wanted Jack. And she couldn't stay one minute longer.

Getting up, she walked around the room to try and find Greyson. He was bouncing from group to group, dancing, playing around, telling jokes, making a mockery of himself. She caught his eye, and he grabbed her arm as she walked near him. "Addison, baby. Let me introduce you." He wrapped his arms around her, holding her tightly.

"Um, I don't feel good. I'm actually going to go. I'm sorry."

"Do you want to go up to the room and rest?"

"No, thank you. I'm going to call a cab and call it a night."

"Reschedule?"

"I appreciate it, but I'm not sure it's going to work out."

"What? Why? Really? Okay, well, your loss. I'll have Rosie do it with me. She's an attractive little thing. Plenty of women want to be on the campaign with me."

Addison squinted her eyes and shook her head. How could he be so disgusting. "Good luck with that." As she started to walk away, she felt a pull to say something to him. Turning back around, she looked at him directly. "You know, I saw a glimmer of hope in you, but you have showed me your true colors. And now I see otherwise. It doesn't matter how good looking you are, if you are not a good person, it's all a wash."

Greyson laughed. "I'll take the good looks. I get what I want. Thanks for the advice."

Addison couldn't believe him. "Point proven. Have a good life. Please let Mr. Lambert know that I quit."

Greyson wasn't fazed. He turned his sights to someone else and began talking and laughing, completely ignoring their conversation and the fact that she was bothered.

Addison pulled out her phone as she began walking out and called a cab. She waited out front until she got picked up. It was a quiet ride back to her apartment, but it was a sigh of relief being away from the likes of those people. Getting home, she spent the rest of New Year's Eve alone in bed watching the countdown. It wasn't spontaneous; it wasn't sparkly and frilly, but it was real. Her soul felt at peace for doing the right thing.

Chapter 12: Back to Edgerton

It was mid-day on January first. It was the first official day of the new year. Addison was sitting in James' driveway. She prayed Jack was still in Edgerton. If not, she would travel to Waterford to see him. Her car was packed, her apartment was for lease, and she didn't have a set plan. She hoped that whatever would come out of this visit would be positive and well received. Nerves had her jittery as she got herself ready to knock on the door. She began to get out of the car, when she saw a man in the distance, walking up from the horse stables. Amongst the frost, with crepuscular rays extending from the clouds above him in the distance, he looked dreamy. The way he was walking, so stern and strong, his muscles toned and flexed, carrying feed to the animals. She couldn't wait to hear his voice and see his smile. She had missed him so.

She walked down to where he was, slowly, so she didn't startle him. She grew anxious, not knowing if her arrival would be something he still wanted.

Jack walked out of the barn and set his sights on her. Surprised, he smiled. "Hi."

Addison smiled. "Hi."

The energy was heightened. The feelings were as strong as ever, maybe even more. It was magnetic. The connection, the attraction, it was undeniable and forceful, passionately seducing one another. Her heart wanted his. His heart wanted hers. They were pounding fiercely for one another.

Addison felt a desire for him that made it hard for her to stand still. It felt so right, she could feel it in her bones. There was an aching in her body that yearned for his embrace. He was the warmth and sense of home that she longed for.

Addison rubbed her lips together before she began to speak. "Um ... so ... have you ever made a mistake?" she asked playfully with a twinge to her voice.

Jack furrowed his brows. "Yeah, of course. All the time."

"I think I made the biggest mistake of my life."

Curious, Jack squinted his eyes. "Oh yeah, what's that?"

"I never should have left."

"I thought you loved New York? What happened to your opportunity?"

"It just didn't feel right. Nothing has felt right since I left. And I think I know why."

"Why?"

"You."

"Me, huh?" Jack moved closer to her. "Explain."

Being close to him made every hair on her body stand up. She desired him in every way imaginable. He was the kindest, most gentle-hearted man she had ever met. Just being near him made her feel safe and calm. As she spoke, she stared at his broody lips, the bottom one full, and the top one thin with a bow shape. Focusing on them made her knees weak. She licked and bit her bottom lip as she scanned them over.

"My car is packed. I couldn't fit everything. I will have to get a mover. I only brought the necessities. My apartment is for lease. I quit my job."

"Wow. That's quite the move. Quite the change. What made you quit?"

"Everything felt wrong. Suddenly, nothing made sense there anymore. When I met you, it was like my whole life made sense. You have been what I have been waiting for, dreaming of, searching for ... I was looking for happiness in the wrong places and wanting the wrong things. I knew I needed to get back here as soon as possible to tell you."

"You want to be a country girl? You think you can do that?"

"I mean, I grew up here. I pretty much am. But if we can make a deal to take a trip into the city maybe once a year, I'd be good with that."

Jack laughed. "Well, we did discuss the idea of compromise. We can look for somewhere in the middle."

"Anywhere with you feels right."

"And you can forgive me for everything?" He looked at her endearingly, needing confirmation that she wasn't holding anger towards him.

Addison stepped even closer to him. Putting her hand to his forehead and swiping his hair to the side, she smiled. She was an inch away from his face. She looked up and stared into his eyes. She had never adored a human being so much. "There's nothing to forgive."

The tension was building. The pull was undeniable.

Addison grabbed the sleeve of his shirt. "I see you are wearing flannel."

Jack looked at her shirt that was peeking out of her jacket. "I see you are too. We are matching again."

"I think that's a sign. Don't you?" she asked.

"Or we just like flannel."

"I did bring my jean shirt. It's in the car."

A smirk formed on Jack's face as he thought about it. "I'll have to buy one."

Addison, wanting him to kiss her, knew she had to give the go ahead. "You know, I never got a New Year's Eve kiss last night."

"You didn't?"

"Nope, I was all alone at midnight. How about you?" Addison clenched her jaw and prayed that he said the same.

"I wasn't alone, but the only kiss I got was from the dog. Dad and I watched the countdown together."

Addison released the tension in her body, hearing that he wasn't with anyone romantically. "I thought about calling you so many times, but I thought seeing you in-person would be better."

"Well, since you didn't get a New Year's Eve kiss, and I didn't get a New Year's Eve kiss... I was thinking ..."

Jack and Addison leaned forward into the most perfect, sensual kiss. It was sweet; it was gentle; it was infused with passion, sending shivers across their bodies, and leaving them in a peaceful and blissful moment. It was like an electrical current moving through their veins. As their lips touched, soft and slightly wet, they closed their eyes and took it in. It was worth the wait. All of the built-up emotion was felt in that kiss. He put his hands on the sides of her face and gently kissed the side of her mouth, under her eye, and on her forehead.

Jack embraced her, holding her in his arms.

"Can I admit something to you?" he asked.

"Yeah, sure."

"I haven't slept in days. I actually got in my car a few times and started heading towards the city to come see you. I just didn't want to disrupt your life. I didn't know if you were angry with me. But letting you go was the hardest thing I've ever done. Basically, Dad and I have been two lost souls, grieving over the women we love. There is something special about the Monroe women."

"Did you say love?"

"I did. If I'm honest, I was taken from the get go. First look at those pretty eyes and that smile of yours … you had me."

Tears filled the inlets of her eyes. She had waited her whole life to hear those words from the right person. She felt complete. It was her destined path to be back in her hometown with the love of her life.

"I love you too. I knew it all along, I just needed to clear my head. I was scared. But I know for sure that you are what I want. I want to be with you. I want a life with you. I want to build a family with you. I want to grow old with you. I want to build things together; I want to make our own garden; I want to cook for you; I want to dance with you, sing with you, tend to the animals with you … I want this. You and me in the country. Love is what's important. Love is the answer. It's the greatest thing in the world, and I want that."

"How can you be sure that you won't grow to dislike it again and want to go back searching for that big dream?"

"That dream wasn't real. It was a fantasy I held onto as a kid. This is real. I have never felt like this before in my entire life. It all makes sense now. You have showed me what life is about, what is important, what real love is. I want a partner. I want a husband. I want a father to my kids. It's not about the location; it's about who I'm with. I can still have dreams and accomplish whatever I want. Like Aunt Wanda said, there's opportunity everywhere; I just have to look for it. My dreams have changed. And they may continue to change. For the better, I hope."

"No more fancy, lavish lifestyle on the upper east side? No modeling career? No billboard?"

"It was a fallacy. It sounded better than it actually was. I was lost, searching for something. But I'm not lost anymore. I found myself when I came back here. I never would have expected it. But it's true."

Jack leaned forward and kissed her for the second time. "I've never wanted anything more."

Addison looked into his eyes. "Somehow, our parents' love brought us together."

"Yeah, I guess it did."

Jack pushed her hair back and slightly pulled on her earlobes, in awe of her earrings and how they sparkled. "They look good on you. I'm glad you are wearing them."

"Oh, that reminds me." Addison reached into her coat pocket and pulled out a square box wrapped in a red bow. "This was supposed to be your Christmas gift. I left too fast; I didn't give it to you."

"You did? What for?" Jack unraveled the wrapping and bow to find a set of sleigh bells inside. He smiled and raised his eyebrows. "Are these the sleigh bells from the store?"

"Yeah, it sold. I figured we could use the luck. You could put them on your office door, or we can find a place together."

"Who needs luck when we have fate."

Addison laughed. "Touché."

Jack grinned. "I need to divulge another piece of information, before we move forward."

Addison tilted her head and raised her eyebrows. "Go on."

"My dad bought the shop."

Addison's mouth fell open and her eyes filled with tears. "No way."

"He may need help figuring out what to do with it."

Addison was filled with joy. She smiled and looked up at the sky. "Merry Christmas, and Happy New Year, Mom," she said out loud. In that moment, everything came full circle. "I guess we will have to figure out what to do with the house too and decide whether or not I should keep it on the market. It is big enough for all of us. There is a great guest house," she hinted.

Jack took in what she was saying. He couldn't believe that she would be so selfless and invite the idea of living with his dad. He pulled her close. "You are extraordinary, Addison Monroe."

"Let's take it one moment at a time and figure it out," she said.

Jack smiled, adoring her new mindset. "I can do that."

They kissed once again. Holding each other, they stood in the pasture, looking out over acres of land, slowly dancing in each other's arms. Sprinkles of snow started to descend at the perfect timing, making it a winter wonder.

Made in the USA
Monee, IL
23 December 2020